Elise

AND

Amos

AND THE

Faerie Stone

uncle Dale

Amanda Boinger   Jess Jenkins

JESS JENKINS

ISBN 978-1-0980-2213-6 (paperback)
ISBN 978-1-0980-2214-3 (digital)

Christian Faith Publishing, Inc.
832 Park Avenue
Meadville, PA 16335
www.christianfaithpublishing.com

Illustrations by Amanda Burgess

Printed in the United States of America

For my roommate—
It took seventeen years, but this is the
book I promised I would write.

And my family—
With the whole gang behind me, anything is possible.

"Elise Alexander, get out of bed this instant!" Elise's grandmother pulled the faded patchwork quilt off the bed and folded it in a few brisk movements. "Your aunt is pacing a hole in my kitchen floor, so you'd best get moving. Take that lazy hound of yours outside so he's ready to go in the car." The flood of words stopped as she paused to scratch the brown-and-white basset hound behind one ear.

He cracked one eye but didn't move.

"Come on, Amos," she said, pulling on his collar. "You've got to get ready to go. Mim has been looking for the perfect house for over five years, and no lazy basset is going to hold her up."

"But I don't want to move, Grams," Elise said. The cheerful yellow walls blurred as she blinked away the tears threatening to overflow. This had been her room for the past five years, since she had come to live with Grams and Aunt Mim when she was seven. After her parents were killed in a car accident, this room had become her safe place in a world that was suddenly very scary.

"I know, honey," said Grams, "but your aunt has been saving for years and waiting for the perfect house, and this might be it. We are the Three Musketeers. We have to stick together."

Elise smiled weakly and nodded, trying to ignore the squeezing pain in her stomach. She could do this as long as they were together. They had been the Three Musketeers ever since Grams had read her the book. Reading with Grams was the last part of getting ready for bed and, to Elise, the most important. The characters in the stories kept her company when she felt alone in her room.

Grams dragged Amos off the bed and sent him down the hall as Elise pulled on some clothes. She sat back down on the bed and closed her eyes, focusing on her breathing the way her therapist taught her. *In, hold, out, relax.* She picked up the photograph of her parents from her bedside stand, where they sat watching over her.

"I don't want to move somewhere you've never been," Elise whispered, her voice catching at the end. Their unchanging smiles stared up at her, and finally, she sighed. "I'll try to think of positive reasons for moving, but I'm not sure there are any." She closed her eyes and tried to make a mental list. "There's still only one good reason," she complained to the picture, managing a small smile. At least it would be fun to live near Uncle Jake. Aunt Mim's impatient voice stopped her list at one reason, and she put the picture back in its place and ran downstairs.

* * * * *

"I think you're going to like this new place," Aunt Mim said, tapping her fingers on the steering wheel. "Jake said it's big and has a great history, whatever that means. Your parents were investors in the bed-and-breakfast idea, and your mother loved her coffee, so you are going to be part owner. You have to give your stamp of approval. Jake has already decided we should get it, but I don't completely trust him. I think he just wants us to move closer to this new university job of his."

Elise's stomach flip-flopped at the thought of going to a new town. That would mean a new school and new places, all where her parents had never been.

"It might be great," Elise said in a small voice, trying to push down the anxiety she felt at the thought of moving. Her grandmother's house was the strongest connection she still had to her parents. "I had a dream that Mom and Dad came to see the house with us," Elise continued. "We were arguing about where to put the Christmas tree like we do every year, but no one could agree because it was a new house."

"Who won?" Grams asked, giving Elise a wink. Elise caught a glimpse of Aunt Mim's frown in the mirror before Grams reached over and squeezed her hand. "Don't frown, Mim. You could use some more time turning your imagination loose!"

"Jake took all of the imagination," Aunt Mim said, rolling her eyes. "I spent my time making sure his imagination didn't leave him with a broken leg somewhere."

"That only happened once," said Grams with a laugh. "You know he just did those things because his little sister always told him not to. The stories I ended up with from the two of you!"

"Let's tell stories," Elise suggested. "Grams first, then Aunt Mim, and then me."

"What kind of story would you like?" Grams asked.

"A true story," said Elise. "Tell me a story about my parents."

Stories in the car always helped pass the time, and, before Elise was completely ready, they were coming into Silverleaf.

* * * * *

"We're almost there," Aunt Mim said. "Jake said it was outside of town just past the Cree-Mee. I've never been past the ice cream shop before."

"He definitely picked a landmark we know!" said Grams. "Wouldn't it be great to be able to walk to get ice cream?"

The house loomed at them suddenly as they came around the bend past the Cree-Mee.

"Goodness!" exclaimed Aunt Mim. "It's bigger than I thought."

They pulled in the curved driveway and got out of the car, their heads tipped back to take in all three stories of the house.

Uncle Jake waved at them from the wide front porch. "What do you think, Mim?" he asked with a grin, bounding down the front steps. "When I heard it was for sale, I knew you should take a look. It's fantastic!"

The house was a pale-yellow stone that seemed to glow in the sunlight. There were three floors with porches and balconies jutting out unexpectedly at all angles. The front porch was high, raised up

nearly six feet off the ground, with a curved walkway disappearing into the shadows under the front steps. The left side of the house had a bay window that stuck out like half of a honeycomb up all three floors, but it was the other side of the house that caught Elise's attention. There was a fairy-tale tower. Arched windows wrapped around the tower, which was topped by a pointed roof, complete with a small tower-shaped chimney. Elise smiled. If they had to move, at least she could live in a tower. She stepped back and took in the whole house.

"It looks like a castle smashed into a farmhouse and got stuck," said Elise.

Uncle Jake laughed and came to look again from beside Elise. "It does sort of look like that," he agreed. "I heard it was built by some crazy Irish prince who lost his land and came to America to start again."

"Why did the last owners leave?" asked Aunt Mim.

"Renters," Uncle Jake corrected. "That," he continued in a dramatic whisper, "is where the story gets interesting."

Aunt Mim rolled her eyes. "Is it haunted?"

"That's what they say," Uncle Jake said, trying to sound casual, but his twinkling eyes gave him away. "There were strange noises, and things kept moving or disappearing. The couple even claimed they heard voices in the tower room, but they never saw a trace of people anywhere."

"Humph," Grams said. "They can say whatever they want as long as that means the price is good."

They were interrupted by another car pulling into the driveway. A woman got out and waved to Uncle Jake. "Good morning," she said briskly. "I am Robin. You must be Miriam." She shook hands with Aunt Mim. "We've been in touch on the phone."

"Please call me Mim," said Aunt Mim. "This is my mother, Emma Alexander, and my niece, Elise." Elise waited for the familiar double take from Robin. She didn't fit in with the family very well. Elise had inherited her mother's dark Cuban coloring, which stood out against her family's pale skin and light hair. She had also inherited one brown eye from her mother and one green eye from her father.

9

People sometimes stared, but Elise liked having this combination of both her parents. Robin just smiled as she shook everyone's hands.

Amos barked. "And this is Amos," Uncle Jake added, stroking the dog's ears. "He thinks he is a person, too." Amos growled at Robin and wagged his tail. "He also likes to pretend he is fierce." Robin let Amos sniff her hand and then scratched his ears. Amos licked her hand before going to investigate the bushes.

"Has Jake been telling you about the house?" Robin asked with a small twinkle in her eye. "I'm sure by now he has mentioned that the last renters thought it was haunted."

"It was one of the first things he told us," Aunt Mim said, ignoring Jake's innocent look.

"Well, let's look inside, and then you can decide if a little unconfirmed haunting is worth the price the seller is asking." Robin led them inside and stopped to let them catch their breaths.

"Wow!" whispered Elise. The entryway was dark wood awash with color from the tall stained-glass windows. Spiral stairs swirled around the edge of the room up to the second floor. The stair railing and the pillars set into the walls were carved with ivy curling its way to the ceiling. Blooming from the ivy were small star-shaped flowers.

"That will take a lot of cleaning," said Grams.

"It's perfect," said Aunt Mim.

"And you haven't even seen the rest of the house," said Uncle Jake with a laugh. "The main kitchen will need some remodeling but could be easily changed to let you bake everything you would need for a coffee shop and still cook meals for people staying over." He pulled them into one of the rooms off to the side. "You can set up the coffee counter here and make these rooms and the porch for the coffee guests."

Robin nodded. "There is a formal dining room in the back that can be used for the resident guests and space for an office as well. The second floor has a number of rooms, some of which have been renovated into a small suite. The third floor is a bit smaller, but you could have three bedrooms, a living area, one full bath, and a kitchenette. If you wanted to live on-site, it would be perfect for the three of you. And, of course, there is the tower room," she said with a wink at Elise.

"Come look at this," Uncle Jake said, pulling Aunt Mim through the house. "It has a solarium." He opened the door with a flourish, and Elise blinked at the sudden brightness. The whole room was made of glass. "You could put in a small fountain and have a garden, even in the winter!" Uncle Jake pulled them into the room as he let his imagination run wild.

"Control yourself," Aunt Mim said, though Elise could see she was considering the possibilities as fast as Uncle Jake was describing them.

They walked through the rest of the first floor with Robin and Uncle Jake pointing out all the interesting features of the house. Robin noticed that Elise was getting restless. "Why don't you explore the rest of the house."

Elise shook her head and grabbed Grams's hand. "Try looking at the second floor," suggested Grams. "We will be up in just a few minutes, and you can always come back down if you want."

Elise made a face but nodded and took a deep breath. It was getting easier to go places on her own, but she had never been in this house before. Uncle Jake walked her over to the bottom of the stairs and smiled encouragingly. "You can do it, cafecito," he said.

Robin smiled at the nickname. "Cafecito?" she asked. "Is that a kind of coffee?"

"Cuban espresso," explained Uncle Jake with a grin. "Small but mighty!"

Elise rolled her eyes but managed a small smile. "Small but mighty," she whispered to herself as she walked up the stairs. She stopped on the landing halfway up and gazed at the curved staircase. This was not the kind of house she had imagined living in. She continued up the stairs, watching the colored lights from the stained-glass window shimmer on the dark wood. It really *was* like a castle here, though probably warmer and homier than she imagined stone castles were.

The second floor was full of bedrooms. This would be where the guests would stay. Elise stopped at the top of the stairs where she could still hear the voices of the adults downstairs. The stairs opened up into a smallish hallway with glass doors at the far end that opened onto a balcony. Elise peeked into each room but did not venture in. The empty spaces echoed unnervingly as she made her way around the curved hallway. There was another set of stairs leading up to the third floor. Elise peeked out a window to the back yard. The garden was wild and overgrown but was bursting with color.

"It's not so bad, Amos," she said over her shoulder. "I think you might even like it here if you give it a chance." She turned to see Amos's reaction, but he wasn't behind her anymore. She heard him bark in one of the bedrooms back around the corner.

"What is it?" she called as she peeked in the door. Her voice echoed off the empty wooden walls. Amos was looking out of a window that was swinging open. Elise pulled him away from the window and peered down through the glass roof of the solarium. "Did you push the window open?" she asked Amos as she pulled it closed. "I guess if there was really a ghost it wouldn't need to open a window to get out." She heard footsteps behind her and turned to find the adults coming.

"These rooms are fantastic!" Aunt Mim exclaimed as she pushed open the door to the adjoining bathroom. "What do you think, Elise?" she asked.

"The window was open," Elise replied. "What if something got in?"

Uncle Jake came over and looked at the window. "I don't think there's any way for a person to climb up," he said. "The solarium is just below, so it would be too hard to get up here." He tousled Elise's hair. "And there is no sign of any animals. I don't think anything came in the window."

"What if something went out?" Elise asked. "What if there really was something in the house?"

Grams laughed and shook her finger at Uncle Jake. "This is what happens when you start telling ghost stories." She took Elise's face in her hands. "There are no ghosts here, Elise. And there is no sign of anything else in the house. Animals would leave signs, and no person could have gone anywhere from that window." She waited until Elise nodded and then led her from the room.

Robin and Aunt Mim came from looking at the rest of the rooms. "I think this place is just what we were looking for," said Aunt Mim. "There are plenty of rooms, and they are set up perfectly. Shall we look at the third floor?"

The group walked around the corner once again and up the stairs. There was a short hallway with two doors and a sitting area with a small kitchenette.

"The tower room is there," Robin said, pointing to another door across the room. She showed the others around the sitting area while Elise walked into the tower room.

Just inside the door was a small squarish room with a closet, and then the room rounded out into the tower. It was small but had a curved window seat all around. The windows looked over the front of the house and out toward the east. "This will be my room, Amos," she said finally. "I suppose it won't be too bad to move if I can live in the tower of a castle."

The adults came in and found Elise. "What do you think, honey?" asked Grams.

"If I can have this room, I say yes," she said.

Aunt Mim smiled. "I suppose you are the princess, so the tower would belong to you. Let's go outside and see the garden."

As they were leaving, there was a small thump and a scuffling noise in the ceiling. "Are there mice?" asked Aunt Mim.

"Very likely," answered Robin. "The house has been empty for a few months, and you're right next to the woods. It shouldn't take too much to get rid of them."

"It sounds bigger than that. More like a rat," suggested Uncle Jake. He laughed as Grams swatted his arm and pushed him out of the room.

"Don't give Elise any ideas," she scolded, glancing at Elise. "She has to sleep in this room."

The group made their way down all the stairs and out the back door. The garden was brimming with the deep reds and purples of foxgloves and mallow, patches of bright orange marigolds, and white honeysuckle climbing wildly over a slanted trellis. Overgrown rose bushes twined together around the back of the house and around a small garden shed on one side of the yard.

"It will take some work to get back into shape, but the garden was well-planned and, as you can see, most of the plants are still thriving," Robin said as the family wandered around the garden. She pointed toward the woods behind the house. "There is a small stream in the back with a bridge and lots of pathways and hidden nooks along the edge of the woods and behind some of the bushes."

Elise looked around while the adults talked. Amos trotted down the path sniffing at the clumps of overgrown flowers before disappearing behind a giant rhododendron. Elise sighed as she followed him. It would be nice to have all this space for Amos. Elise found a stone bench hidden behind the bush and sat down to make a mental list of all the positive things about the house.

She didn't want to leave her old house, but she knew that Aunt Mim really wanted to move here. She stroked Amos's long ears. "I guess we can make the best of it for one of the musketeers." Suddenly, Amos barked and ran down the path. Elise caught a glimpse of something diving into a thick clump of hostas. She followed Amos, who was sniffing and smashing his way through the plants where the creature had disappeared.

"It must have been a rabbit," she said.

Amos growled and plowed through another clump of hostas. Elise followed him as well as she could on the path. She couldn't see any tracks, but Amos must have caught the scent of something. He sneezed and continued pushing through the flowers toward the woods. They crossed the bridge and turned a corner. Amos stopped and growled.

The clearing was pushed back into the trees, out of sight of the house. There were no flowers here, just a circle of stones set in the overgrown grass. Elise walked around the circle as Amos sniffed the stones suspiciously. Here, the ground was not so hard, but Elise still couldn't see any tracks in the long grass.

"What do you think it was, Amos?" Elise asked.

Amos snorted and sniffed around the circle again. He ran back and forth between the circle and the forest a few times and then wandered into the brush between the clearing and the house.

Elise heard Uncle Jake calling.

"I'm back here," she answered. "Come and look at this!"

Uncle Jake followed her voice. "A Faerie Ring!" he exclaimed. "This must be something that he brought from Ireland."

"Who?" asked Elise. "And what's a Faerie Ring?"

"The original builder," said Uncle Jake. "A Faerie Ring is supposed to be a passageway to the Faerie Realm. They were believed to be quite dangerous. If you went into one by mistake, you could get stuck there." They started walking back to the house. "The Faerie would also steal children and make them slaves in the Faerie Realm. If you get stuck there, never eat or drink anything from the Faerie. If you do, you will be trapped there forever."

"What nonsense are you telling her now?" asked Aunt Mim.

"Just warning her of the dangers of associating with the Faerie," said Uncle Jake with a grin. "You have a Faerie Ring in the back. I don't want her to get stuck in the Faerie Realm."

Aunt Mim rolled her eyes. "I'm pretty sure that won't be a problem," she said, smiling at Elise before getting back to business. "This house is better than I hoped for," she said, rubbing her hands together. She turned to Grams. "We could do a lot with this place, and we have Jake close by to help us." She grinned as he started to protest. "It will be fun," she insisted. "And you will be guaranteed free coffee for life."

"Well, in that case, I guess I could come by once in a while to help," he agreed. "I also have some students who could use some work this summer. We can have this place ready in no time!" Just then, there was a thump and a small shriek. A snake slithered out of the lilies and across the path. The lilies rustled in a wobbly line leading toward the house.

"What made that noise?" asked Elise. "It sounded like someone shouting." She looked in the flowers where the sound came from but didn't see anything.

Uncle Jake smiled. "Maybe you have garden ghosts," he said, winking at Elise as they started back toward the house.

"There's no such thing," Elise said with a laugh.

Grams shook her head at their nonsense. "This garden is going to be a lot of work, and that's a fact." She looked at Elise and raised one eyebrow. "What do you think, Elise? Should we give it a shot?"

Elise looked at Aunt Mim's excited face and nodded. "We're the Three Musketeers," she said, pushing down the lurking feeling of panic. "All for one."

"If you're the musketeers, what does that make me?" asked Uncle Jake, trying to look hurt.

"The damsel in distress," shot back Aunt Mim. "Sadly accurate most days."

Uncle Jake made a face as Elise giggled. "Sisters..." he sighed to Elise in a loud whisper.

"Now, now, children," Grams said with a fake sigh. "They've been like this since they could both talk," she said to Robin. "Let's stay focused. I'm in. I haven't had this much garden to play in ever!"

Aunt Mim nodded and shook Robin's hand. "We'll take it," she said.

Elise called for Amos. He hadn't followed them back from the clearing. He came trotting up the path wagging his tail. "You seem very pleased with yourself," Uncle Jake said as he scratched Amos's ears. "Did you find something good back there?"

Amos licked his hand and looked smug. He sniffed the air and then jumped at the nearest clump of flowers. They shook, and Elise watched a trail of plants wave as something ran through the garden. Maybe this place was haunted after all.

The next two weeks crept by. Aunt Mim was busy calling people and filling out forms. Grams was busy sorting and packing anything they weren't using. Elise refused to pack a single sock until the final papers were signed.

"I know I have to do it," she told Amos one evening. "But I feel, somehow, that moving will change everything. It will make them really gone." She looked at her parents smiling at her from their place on the nightstand. "I know they're not coming back, but sometimes, I imagine that I'm just staying here while they're on vacation, like before. Once we move, I can't even imagine that anymore." She laid her head on Amos's side, his warm fur tickling her cheek. The door creaked open, and Aunt Mim stuck her head in.

"How's it going?" she asked, sitting on the floor beside Elise. She looked around the room and then at the two on the floor. She stroked Amos's head. "I signed the final papers today," she said softly. "It's going to take a bit of time to get everything ready to go, but it looks like we will be moving just after school gets out next week."

Elise felt the familiar squeezing feeling rising in her stomach. She tried to take a deep breath, but there wasn't enough space for her lungs to work properly. She nodded and tried not to cry. Aunt Mim was so excited about this move, and she didn't want to ruin it for her.

Aunt Mim wasn't fooled. "It's okay to be upset," she said. Elise looked at her with surprise. "I heard you talking to Amos," Aunt Mim explained with a small smile. "I know you think I don't understand your imagination, and I do worry sometimes that you imagine too much that your parents will come back." She paused and stroked Elise's hair. "Sometimes, I imagine it, too," she confessed. "I would love for it to be true. I miss your parents. Especially now. Your father was a great older brother. He was the one who encouraged me to start this business. He knew it was my dream. He invested a lot of money in it, and he and your mother were always looking out for houses that would be good."

Aunt Mim smiled at the picture on the nightstand and then sighed. "They would have loved this new house." She shook her head and looked back at Elise. "I know it will be hard to move. If you don't want to pack up your room, you can go stay with Uncle Jake, and Grams and I will do it for you. We will unpack all your things in your new room, and you can come to the new house with everything all set up. What do you think?"

Elise thought for a minute but finally shook her head. "I think I should do it," she finally said. "It will be like saying goodbye to all the memories of them that are here." She felt a tear fall into Amos's fur. "It might take me a while to do it though," she admitted.

"Take all the time you need," Aunt Mim said, kissing the top of her head. "We have a lot of stuff to sort through in this house, and we still have the storage container. We kept a lot of the things from your parents' old house. You can choose where to put them in the new house. It will be like your mom and dad having a part in the coffee shop just like we all dreamed."

Elise sniffed but smiled. She couldn't imagine Aunt Mim daydreaming. But it was good to know that there would be pieces of her parents' life having important places in their new home.

* * * * *

After that, life accelerated into a flurry of packing and planning. School was going to let out next Wednesday, and they planned to move the weekend after. Grams insisted the house had to be cleaned from top to bottom before they moved in, and Aunt Mim decided to repaint some of the rooms.

"I'll go stay with Jake for a few days while we try to finish some of these jobs," said Aunt Mim. "I will take care of the cleaning and painting and then come back to help finish up packing."

Grams laughed. "That will be the best motivation for both of you to get the house finished," she said with a wink to Elise. "I expect everything will be ready in just a few days!"

There were a few snags, but Aunt Mim soldiered on. At first, she was determined she and Jake would do it all by themselves, but after the first day, Uncle Jake convinced her to hire some of his university students who had just finished school for the summer. They finished the painting in record time, and Grams and Elise came for the final day of cleaning. The only places Grams allowed them to skip were the attics.

"There will be plenty of time for that when we are ready to move things up there," she said as Elise and Aunt Mim shared a knowing grin behind her back.

Finally, the last box was moved from their old house to the new. Aunt Mim sighed as she slouched in her big armchair. "Whew! We had more stuff than we realized," she said to Grams.

"I realized how much you had," grumbled Uncle Jake from his place on the couch. "I told you it would take a small army to move all your things."

"Well, since you had an army available, I wasn't worried," retorted Aunt Mim.

"Yes, your students were just the force we needed," said Grams, recognizing an argument brewing. "Now, we get to unpack and start making lists of things we need to fill up all the guest rooms. We have to think of themes and names for them all, too!"

"That sounds like my cue to head home," Uncle Jake said, pulling himself to his feet. He hesitated and motioned for everyone to listen. "I swear I hear something scurrying through the ceiling," he muttered, "but every time I try to listen, there isn't anything there."

"If there are mice, we can trap them," said Aunt Mim. "I'm not too concerned about it."

* * * * *

The next morning, however, she was definitely more concerned. There were crumbs on the counter, and some of the crockery had been shifted.

"Do mice like coffee?" she asked as Elise came into the main room. "I know I cleaned the counters last night, but there are crumbs and coffee grounds all over this morning. I've never heard of mice eating coffee."

"Maybe you or Grams spilled it and didn't realize there was so much," suggested Elise.

"Maybe," Aunt Mim muttered. "We have to get this sorted out quickly. We will have to be inspected before we are allowed to open, and if there are mice, I'm pretty sure no one is going to want to order any food here. Maybe the contractors will find something downstairs. They are coming this afternoon to get started."

She cleaned up the counter, muttering to herself. Elise smiled. Aunt Mim was on a mission. These mice didn't know what they were up against.

Aunt Mim found some mouse traps and set them around the kitchen. Amos steered clear. He had had a run-in with mousetraps once when he was a puppy and stayed far away from them now.

* * * * *

When they checked the kitchen the following morning, there were a few dried cranberries on the floor, but the traps were untouched.

"I know those weren't there last night," said Aunt Mim. "The package is sealed, and there aren't any holes. I don't know how they are resealing the package." She whirled around, brandishing the cranberries. "Is one of you sleepwalking?" she demanded of Grams and Elise.

"Never have in my life," replied Grams. "Maybe we have very clever mice. Or rats. Like the Rats of NIMH, right Elise?" Grams smiled, remembering one of the books she had read to Elise when she was younger.

"I've always wanted a NIMH rat," Elise agreed. "Maybe we can catch it on camera."

"Maybe we will just close everything up tighter," said Aunt Mim. "If they can't get any food, they will leave soon." She motioned to the piles of boxes stacked around the room. "We have a lot of work to do today. Let's finish up the third floor and get ourselves comfortable, then we can start working on the rest of the house."

Elise enjoyed the day arranging and rearranging the furniture in their new home. With two rooms, she had more space than before, so Aunt Mim gave Elise her mother's rocking chair. It was a large comfortable chair, and Grams gave her a blanket to put over the back.

"Just be careful of Amos's tail," she warned. "He's not going to fit on your lap in this chair, and he will be jealous."

They took turns helping each other arrange their bedrooms and, after a long day of working, sat down at their small table for dinner.

"It is starting to feel like home," Grams said cheerfully. "We'll have to get some groceries and have a nice meal tomorrow to celebrate."

"If the mice don't get into all the groceries first," Aunt Mim said with a grimace. "I'm going to start working on that tonight!" She spent the evening muttering to herself in the kitchen. She put food in plastic containers or moved bags and boxes to higher shelves in the cupboards. "There are no holes in the cupboards, so they must be getting in some other way," she said. "We'll see if anything goes missing tonight."

"Speaking of going missing," Grams said, "has anyone seen my prism suncatcher? I miss having my rainbows in my room."

"I haven't," said Elise.

"Neither have I," said Aunt Mim. "It must still be in a box somewhere. We'll probably be finding things in boxes for a while longer. Watch out for the traps," she reminded Elise as she started getting ready for bed. "No midnight snacks!"

* * * * *

Elise was the first one awake the next morning. She turned the corner to the kitchen and froze. The counters were clean, but the traps were spread out like a minefield between the sink and the table. If one of them had come out in the night, she would have gotten a nasty surprise.

"Something strange is happening, Amos," Elise said as she put the traps back. "I'm not sure we should let Aunt Mim see this. She is stressed out enough without rats that set traps for humans." She looked around. Everything else seemed to be as they had left it. "We have to get a camera," Elise said.

* * * * *

When Uncle Jake dropped by a few days later to help in the garden, Elise told him about their plan to catch the clever rats on camera.

"So we are up to rats now, are we?" he asked with a laugh. "Mim must love that."

"Maybe they are like the rats from the Rats of NIMH, and they are just very intelligent," Elise explained. "They leave the bait, but the traps are set off or the whole trap is moved to a different spot. They must be really smart to be able to do that without getting caught at all. Do you have a camera we could use to catch them in the act?"

"I don't, but one of my colleagues might," Uncle Jake said with a smile. "This sounds like a job for the science department! I'll ask Henry if he has something that would work for this."

* * * * *

Uncle Jake came back the following evening with a coworker from the science department. "This is Dr. Henry Sproule, one of the science professors," he said. "He can set up a camera and see what is coming in for snacks at night."

Dr. Sproule set up the camera, and Aunt Mim gave him some dessert.

"Thank you so much for this," she said. "We have no idea what is causing these problems. It's not like any mouse that I've ever heard of before. We tried traps but none of them worked. At first, they just ignored them, but then, they were set off, but we never caught anything."

"Mice can learn," Dr. Sproule reassured her. "If people have tried traps before, they may have learned how to avoid them."

"NIMH rats," Grams said with a laugh.

"Which rats?" Dr. Sproule asked.

"It's from a book," explained Uncle Jake. "Fiction. You should read it. Super-intelligent, escaped lab rats who are now living in a rat civilization under a farmhouse." He winked at Elise. "Seems reasonable." He grinned at Dr. Sproule, who sighed and shook his head.

"I will leave that kind of fiction to the English department," said Dr. Sproule. "I'll be back in the morning to check the video and see what we have!"

* * * * *

The next morning, however, Dr. Sproule was puzzled. "There's definitely something here," he muttered as he watched the video for the fifth time. He pointed at the blob of color moving around the screen. "You can see the heat signature, but it isn't in the shape of anything I know." He scowled and rewound the video again. "The heat signature is in a circle, not in the shape of anything specific. It should look like something," he said in frustration. "And this!" He pointed to a small red circle that was moving in short erratic spurts around the room. "This is a floating circle." He glared at the shape darting across the screen.

Elise watched the glowing red circles move around the kitchen. The small one went in and out of the camera's range while the larger one would sometimes blink out like it was invisible, even to the camera.

"It's moving too directly," Dr. Sproule finally said, pointing at the large circle. "A mouse or rat would wander a bit, checking things out here and there. This thing doesn't waste any time. It comes in, goes for the food it wants, and then leaves. It seems like it's intelligent." He looked apologetically at Aunt Mim. "I don't know what it is."

"Well, thank you for trying," Aunt Mim said, handing him a cup of coffee. "We will just have to put our food in tins or other containers that close tightly."

As they discussed the strange nature of the intruders, Grams and Uncle Jake came in. "Well, Henry, what have you found?" asked Uncle Jake. He and Grams listened carefully while Dr. Sproule showed them the video and explained the strange behavior of the frustrating circles.

"Well, if it isn't mice or rats, what other possible explanations are there?" asked Grams. "Squirrels?"

"No, squirrels aren't nocturnal," replied Dr. Sproule.

"Raccoons?" asked Elise.

"No, they are louder and leave more of a mess," said Grams. "You're awfully quiet, Jake. What are you thinking?"

"Something that our esteemed professor would never believe," Uncle Jake said with a grin. "It could be Brownies."

"Brownies?" Dr. Sproule asked in disbelief. "I'm assuming you mean the imaginary ones, as opposed to the snacks. Although both are equally ridiculous."

Uncle Jake laughed. "You have never proven to my satisfaction that the Little People don't exist."

Dr. Sproule shook his head. "I will leave fantasy to the English department. We in science will stick to measurable facts. You know the existence of these beings is just fairy tales."

Uncle Jake shrugged. "The stories have to come from somewhere. You never know what you might find if you are willing to look for it."

"Well, until we get more proof that there are Brownies, Elves, or Fairies in our house, we will just close up the food and set more traps," said Aunt Mim. "There's no sense arguing about something that can't be proven one way or the other."

"But you said this house was built by a crazy Irishman," said Elise. "Maybe they came with him when he built the house!"

"That seems reasonable," agreed Uncle Jake with a wink. "Perhaps they came out of the Faerie Ring."

"No, it does not seem reasonable," argued Dr. Sproule. "All it proves is that people are unduly influenced in their beliefs by the history of the house, and furthermore—"

"Furthermore, it doesn't matter one way or the other," finished Aunt Mim. "Let's get to work. We have enough to do without worrying about the possible existence of mythical creatures in our house." She rubbed her hands together. "Let's get started. Jake and Elise, you go through the attics and see if there is anything useful in them. We will take anything good downstairs, and then, we can put all our boxes in the attic and get them out of the way. Grams and I will start in the garden."

Dr. Sproule finished his coffee with a gulp and hurried out, obviously worried that he might get a job if he stayed any longer.

Jake saluted and took Elise off to explore the attics. There were two, one above the spiral stairs, and the other next to Aunt Mim's room at the top of the stairs. They decided to start in the big attic next to Aunt Mim's room.

"Do you really think there are Brownies in our house?" asked Elise as she and Amos followed Uncle Jake. "Do you think they could be real?"

"The stories certainly came from somewhere," he replied. "People think they were just stories to explain natural events or funny stories someone made up to entertain or scare children, but it seems like the evidence fits the explanation." He paused. "Although, in the stories, Brownies were always helpful to humans. It doesn't seem like Brownies would leave this kind of mess."

"Why was Dr. Sproule so against believing in them?" Elise asked.

"He doesn't want to believe in the stories," Uncle Jake explained. "It's not really that he is a scientist and I'm an English professor who studies legends, but that he has a very ordered mind and doesn't want it messed up with ideas of Faerie creatures." He laughed. "Some people are just like that. They only believe what makes sense to them without allowing for the possibility that there is much more to the world than we can ever know."

"Do you want there to be Brownies in our attic?" Elise asked.

"I would love it!" exclaimed Uncle Jake. "But if there are, I doubt I would see them. You have a much better chance of meeting them than I do. And Amos might be the first one to know for sure, but for now…" He paused and waved his hand toward the attic.

They turned to take stock of the task in front of them. There were boxes and bits of furniture piled haphazardly around the room. "Mim will have a heyday up here," muttered Uncle Jake as he picked up a dusty box bristling with wooden candlesticks. "There is some good stuff here, though." He sighed. "I guess we'll start making piles of things that Mim might want to take down and use." He grabbed the end of a large headboard and grunted as he lifted it. "But it will take more strength than we have to get some of this furniture downstairs. "Let's see if we can shift some of the good stuff nearer the stairs."

As they moved boxes and uncovered more bits of furniture, Elise secretly looked for evidence of Brownies. She finally admitted to herself that she didn't know what she was looking for. She would have to do some research before she could investigate further.

Elise and Uncle Jake had worked their way to the back corner of the attic, shifting side tables and old chairs out of the way.

"I wonder where all this stuff came from," said Elise. "Some of it looks really old, but other stuff is much newer."

"One of the previous renters must have been a collector of some kind," replied Uncle Jake. "I wonder why they didn't take it when they moved."

They worked a while longer before Uncle Jake called a rest. "We should check out the other attic before lunch. We should also check your room. There seem to be attics all over this house, and I bet there is some kind storage above your room as well. Who knows what we might find in the tower!"

A quick tour of the attic above the stairs revealed only broken furniture, an old trunk, and some boxes covered with spider webs and dust.

"It looks like most of the good stuff is in the other attic. Let's report to your aunt and see what she wants to do with everything," suggested Uncle Jake.

They called the others in for lunch and reported their findings to Aunt Mim. She and Grams decided to spend the afternoon helping in the attic. "We can start putting furniture in the guest rooms," Aunt Mim said with glee. "If we don't have to buy furnishings for all those rooms, we may be able to open sooner than I thought!"

All afternoon, Aunt Mim and Uncle Jake shifted boxes and carried bed frames, a few dressers, a plethora of side tables, chairs, and other bits of furniture down to the second floor, while Grams and Elise washed and organized things into groups.

"There's more than I imagined up there," Aunt Mim said with a sigh. "Some of these tables and chairs can go downstairs, and we still have enough to furnish most of two rooms and some of the family suite. At this rate, we could be open by the time families are bringing their kids to school in the fall!"

Grams smiled. "The garden will take some work, but it can be artistically overgrown the first year. It is still beautiful even with everything growing every which way."

"That just leaves the rest of the coffee shop and remodeling the kitchen and coffee counter to get sorted," said Aunt Mim. "We need to find a bunch more tables and chairs, some comfortable chairs for the lounge room, and some tables for the outdoor seating."

"Is that all?" Uncle Jake asked with a laugh. "For having such a long list, you are still very optimistic about opening early. But," he added as Aunt Mim glared at him, "it just so happens there is a shop that just opened up in town that may have some things you need. It's owned by a man named Kevan Foley. It's full of stuff. If he doesn't have it, he can probably tell you where to find it."

"We'll go in tomorrow," Aunt Mim said.

"Before you go, can you help me look for the door in my room?" Elise asked Uncle Jake.

"What door?" asked Aunt Mim.

"There seems to be an attic in every available space, so I think there might be a trapdoor in her ceiling," explained Uncle Jake. "Are you sure you want to look tonight? What if we open it and can't get it shut again? There could be evil Pixies or Elves in your room!"

"Stop trying to scare her," Grams said, shaking her finger at him. "I'm sure there's nothing dangerous up there, but it might let in some mice or even bats."

"If we can't close it, I'll just sleep in the living room!" Elise said. "Please? I won't be able to sleep at all unless I know if there is something there."

"Fine," said Aunt Mim. "If Jake wants to look, he can, but you are responsible to clean up any mess he makes."

"It looks like I have been volunteered," Jake said, making a face at his sister. "I'm supposed to be the older, bossy one, you know," he said with a fake sigh.

"I grew up faster than you," replied Aunt Mim, tousling his hair with a sweet smile.

Everyone, including Amos, went back up the stairs to Elise's room. Uncle Jake looked all around the ceiling in the round tower room and then went back into the square room and stuck his head in the closet.

"Found it," he said. "It is in a rather inconvenient spot and is pretty small. I don't think there is anything stored up there after all. Maybe it's just roof access. The person would have to be pretty small, though." He pointed to the small framed area of the ceiling. "It is just a board that drops into place. It shouldn't be too hard to get open." He put on his gloves and a filter mask. "Just in case there is insulation or something up there I don't want to breathe," he said to Elise, who had watched him gear up with alarm.

Uncle Jake climbed up on a chair and pushed the wooden board to one side. He stuck his head up and looked around. Elise waited impatiently until he came back down and gave his report.

"It's a very interesting setup. On one side, there is a small door that gives access to the roof, and on the other side, it opens into the tower attic. There are a few boxes up there. I can't tell what's in them. There is a window on the far side, but it's pretty dirty and doesn't let much light in. I didn't see any signs of mice or bats, so it looks pretty safe. The last person to live here must have been pretty small, because it looks like the boxes are stacked, not just pushed in through the hole."

Elise gave him a hug. "Thanks for looking. I'll have to check it out sometime!"

"But not tonight," said Aunt Mim, herding them all out of the room. "Right now, we all need to clean up and have something to eat. This has been a long day, and we need to rest up for tomorrow!"

* * * * *

Elise lay in bed that night thinking about everything they had learned that day. She wondered what Dr. Sproule's mysterious circles could be. Maybe if the camera couldn't capture the creature, she could catch it by surprise. She nudged Amos with her foot. "Should we go see if we can find something in the kitchen, Amos?"

He opened one eye but then shut it again without moving. He was definitely not interested; however, when Elise got up and put on her slippers, he stretched and shuffled after her.

Elise got her flashlight and stuck her head out the door to make sure everyone was in bed. She and Amos crept out and peeked around the corner into the main room. Everything seemed to be just like they had left it. Aunt Mim had carefully wiped the counters and had made Elise check to make sure they were perfectly clean before they went to bed.

"You are my witness," she had said severely. "In the morning, we are going to check this together to see if anything has changed."

Elise hesitated. The moonlight cast wavering black shadows through the windows. The counters were clear, and the traps were all set in their places. She didn't want to sit in the kitchen all night, but it looked like whatever was stealing their food was going to come later. She grabbed a blanket and curled up at the end of the couch. She could see the whole kitchen without being seen.

She waited. After an hour, she lay her head back to rest her eyes. She rested her feet on Amos's side to keep them warm. Suddenly, she felt him raise his head. She stroked him with her foot to keep him quiet and strained her ears to hear what he had heard.

As she stared into the kitchen, she noticed a strange bluish light glowing outside the bay windows. There was a blue spark, and then the window swung silently open. A small creature climbed in the window and stopped on the sill to look around. It motioned to someone outside and then climbed down to the bench and under the table. A second, larger figure climbed in behind it. The blue light flitted back and forth around the kitchen.

"Hurry up," a small grumpy voice came from the kitchen. "And don't forget the coffee."

Elise clapped her hand over her mouth to stifle a gasp of surprise. Amos growled softly, and the creatures froze.

"It's just the dog," said a different voice. "Get ready in case you need to do something about him."

Elise watched as the two shapes climbed nimbly up the drawer handles and looked around the counter. The taller shape softly opened the cupboard doors and Elise blinked as the smaller shape jumped lightly up into the cupboards. It passed tins and bags down to the other one, who opened each one and poured a bit into smaller bags taken from the sack it had carried over its shoulder. Then it passed the containers back up to the one in the cupboard. It seemed Aunt Mim was going to need a different plan to keep these creatures out of the food.

Elise waited until the blue light was hovering near the window before sneaking off the couch. She tiptoed over and flipped on the light, squinting her eyes at the sudden brightness. Through her squinched-up eyes, she saw the figures freeze. Amos growled softly, and they glanced at him before turning to face Elise.

"Who are you?" she asked. "Are you Brownies?"

The smaller creature snorted. "Of course not. I am a Leprechaun," he said with a bow. He had bright red hair and dark green clothes. His round face looked like it should be smiling but was set in a frown. He turned to the blue light. "You were supposed to be keeping watch!"

"I can't see everything," the grumpy voice replied.

Elise jumped and turned to look more closely at the blue light, which had come to rest on the table. It was a tiny man. Everything about him seemed to be pointed. He had small, pointed ears and a long, pointed nose. His pointed chin was covered with a pointed beard. Even his hair, which stuck up around his head, was pointed. She gaped at the shimmery wings on his back, jumping when he snapped at her.

"Yes, I'm a Fairy, and I have wings. Not all Fairies are women." He stared at Elise, daring her to contradict him. His pointed ears quivered with annoyance.

"Well," she said carefully, "I guess it's logical that there would be boy Fairies, too." She looked at the third member of this unusual group. It was small man, a few inches taller than the Leprechaun. His hair and eyes were brown, and his skin was nearly the same shade as Elise's light brown coloring. He looked like a miniature human except for very long pointed ears that stuck up on either side of his cap.

The small man bowed. "I am Tíreachán," he began before the Leprechaun cut him off.

"Don't tell her anything," he commanded. He looked at the Fairy. "Laisrén, magic her, and let's get going. No one needs to know she saw us." When Tíreachán started to protest, the Leprechaun interrupted him again. "Stop or I'll have him magic you, too. Grab the bag. We're going."

He jumped out of the cupboard and climbed down the drawer handles, squeaking in surprise as Amos jumped on him. Amos caught the back of the Leprechaun's coat and gave a firm shake, lifting his head so the Leprechaun's feet were dangling just off the floor.

The Fairy pulled out a short sword and pointed it at Amos. The tip was glowing blue, and Elise realized it must be his wand.

"Wait," she whispered fiercely. "Everyone, stop. We can't make any more noise, or someone will hear." She turned to Amos. "Let him go." She waited until Amos dropped the Leprechaun and then turned to Tíreachán, who had been silent this whole time. "Who are you, and what are you doing in our kitchen?"

The man looked at the Leprechaun, almost like he was asking permission to speak. There was a long moment of silence. Finally, the Fairy broke the silence. "Just tell her. She's caught us fair and square. We can always magic her later if we want to."

The Leprechaun shrugged. He bowed with a little mocking flourish and waved vaguely at the others. "I'm Meallán, the Fairy is Laisrén, and Tíreachán has already told you his name. We are simple travelers passing through on our way to the Faerie Realm."

Tíreachán started to speak, but Meallán cut him off again. "Now, unless there was something you wanted, we will be on our way. Perhaps it would be best if you don't mention meeting us to the big humans. We won't tell if you won't," he finished with a cheeky grin.

Elise nodded. She couldn't imagine trying to explain this to Aunt Mim. "But you have to stop making a mess." She pointed to the bits of food spilled across the counter. "Aunt Mim is going crazy trying to figure out what is going on."

Meallán smirked, but Tíreachán finally managed to speak. "We will try," he said quickly, before anyone could interrupt him. "We don't want to make this any harder."

"Enough," said the Fairy. "Just pretend you've never seen us, and everything will be fine." He turned to the others. "Let's go before they get suspicious."

Before Elise could ask who else there was that might get suspicious, the Fairy flew out the window. The Leprechaun gave another cheeky grin as he bowed and clambered up the bench and out the window. Tíreachán looked apologetically at her as he carried the bag down the drawer handles and toward the window. He stopped on the ledge and turned back, but before he could say anything, the Fairy waved his wand, and the window closed with a soft thud, nearly knocking the small man off the sill. He glanced back through the window before disappearing.

Elise stood looking at the closed window until Amos's cold nose nudged her hand. "What do we do now, Amos?" She sighed and quickly cleaned off the counters. This was not the time to have Aunt Mim searching the house. She walked back to her room thinking about what she would tell Aunt Mim and Grams. Aunt Mim was not going to believe this. "I'm not sure how I'm going to explain this," she said to Amos as she climbed back into bed. "I'll explore the attic tomorrow and see if we find anything."

The next morning, Elise and Amos came out to breakfast later than normal. As she opened her bedroom door, Elise heard Aunt Mim talking to Grams.

"I'm worried about Elise," her aunt was saying. "I know this move has been hard, and she seems to be doing well. I'm just worried that she is taking Jake's ridiculous stories about Brownies a bit too seriously. I know she has a great imagination, and that's wonderful, but I'm a little worried what she may begin imagining next."

"She is fine, Mim," Grams said. "It is normal for her to pretend sometimes that her parents are not gone. She isn't going to get lost in some fantasy. She is too well-grounded for that. Let her have fun with Jake. We'll just have to make sure he doesn't tell her anything too scary."

Elise shut her door silently and thought for a moment. This didn't seem like the right time to tell Aunt Mim about what she saw last night. Maybe she could find some better evidence, and then Aunt Mim might believe her. She opened the door with a bang and called to Amos. "Let's go, Amos. You have to walk down a lot of stairs to go out now." She came around the corner with a smile.

"Did you sleep well?" asked Aunt Mim. "You look a little tired."

"Yes, I slept fine," answered Elise. "I was just up a little late thinking about whatever it is that is making a mess in the kitchen."

"Well, there was no mess this morning, so maybe it has moved on," said Aunt Mim cheerfully. "I just hope it stays gone. We can't afford to have rats if we want to open a coffee shop. No one would come! Take Amos down, and I'll make some French toast."

Elise just nodded and herded Amos down the stairs. This was definitely not the time to tell Aunt Mim that there were two tiny people climbing the drawer handles and opening the cupboards while a Fairy kept watch. When she came back upstairs, Aunt Mim gave her a plate of French toast dripping with syrup.

"I'm going into town this morning to find the shop Jake told us about," Aunt Mim said. "Do you want to come along? We could walk around the town and see what else there is to do here."

"Yes," Elise answered. "Maybe we could see if they have a library."

"I'm sure they have one somewhere," said Aunt Mim. "We'll go in search of it."

Grams decided to come along as well, so the three of them set out to explore their new town. It took about ten minutes to walk to town, and they took turns pointing out things that they saw.

"I can't believe we haven't been to the Cree-Mee yet!" said Grams. "We will definitely need to go there soon."

"Like on the way back?" asked Aunt Mim with a grin.

"Perhaps," said Grams with a sniff. "For all your complaining about stopping for ice cream, you always manage to buy some."

Elise giggled. They all loved ice cream, but Grams had a special love for small ice-cream shops. She had worked at one when she was young and still told stories about it.

They walked slowly down Main Street and looked at the different shops. Finally, they saw the shop that Uncle Jake had told them about. There were tables and chairs scattered around the room with things piled on them seemingly at random. Along the walls were shelves covered with clocks, vases, and other knickknacks. The bell jangled as they pushed the door opened.

A tall man with reddish hair came out from the back room and smiled. "Good morning, lovely ladies! Welcome to my humble establishment. Is there anything I can help you find?" He smiled as Grams looked pointedly around the shop. "Don't worry, ma'am. Despite appearances, I know where everything is, down to the last vase!" He winked at Elise and smiled grandly at Aunt Mim. "But you are the one who is looking for something in particular."

"Yes," replied Aunt Mim. "I'm opening a bed-and-breakfast and coffee shop and need some furniture."

"I have some fine tables and chairs," offered the man. "They are small sets and don't match each other, but I can show you what I have." He waved his hand toward the back of the shop. "You wouldn't happen to be the lady who bought the Irish mansion, would you?"

Aunt Mim nodded. "Yes, I am Miriam Alexander. This is my mother, Emma, and my niece, Elise."

"Lovely to meet you all," the man said with a bow. "My name is Kevan Foley. Welcome to town and to my modest establishment. You will need fair amount to kit that place full out."

"Yes," agreed Aunt Mim. "Do you know the house?"

The man laughed. "That I do. My great-great-grandfather built that house in a bit of folly. He came over from Ireland to make his fortune and did that with his usual flair. Sadly, the flair dwindled through the generations, and my father, who was a real chancer, lost the lot in poor investments. I went back to Ireland with my mother after he died and have only recently come back to sell the house and open this place."

"Why did you sell the house?" asked Elise.

"Well, young lady," he said, "mostly because it's too big for me, and I didn't have such big dreams as your aunt."

"Is it really haunted?" interrupted Elise. "Uncle Jake says it is."

Kevan smiled. "That would be Jake Alexander, the esteemed literature professor?" he asked.

"Yes. He said it is haunted."

"Well, there have been those claims. I don't think there are any ghosts up there though. It isn't old enough, and there haven't been any mysterious accidents. No respectable ghost would take up residence in such a new place."

Elise nodded. She wasn't worried about ghosts but something much more solid. "What about Fairies or Leprechauns? Would those kinds of things live in a new house?" Elise tried to act nonchalant but caught Aunt Mim giving Grams a knowing look. "Are they a little like ghosts?" It seemed that Kevan was about to answer when Aunt Mim interrupted.

"I'm sure there are no ghosts or Little People roaming our house at night," she said, flourishing her list. "If you would be so kind as to show me what furniture you have here, I have a list of items I am looking for."

Kevan smiled and looked at her list. "I have a lot of this and have some ideas where you could find the rest." He walked off with Aunt Mim, pointing out different items, but looked back over his shoulder and grinned. Perhaps, he did know something about Little People after all.

* * * * *

After Aunt Mim's very successful shopping trip at Kevan Foley's store and a stop for ice cream on the way back, Elise was ready to explore the tower attic.

"Here," said Grams, handing her a cloth. "If you clean off the window, you'll be able to see without having to use a flashlight all the time."

"And something will be cleaner than it was before?" asked Elise with a grin.

"We like things to be clean," said Grams, returning the smile. "It doesn't matter if anyone will see it or not."

Elise set up a chair in her closet but found that she still couldn't quite reach the trapdoor. She found a sturdy box to put on top and eyed her tower critically. She looked at Amos. "I suppose there isn't much danger of it falling," she said finally. "It's stuck pretty tightly in the closet." She climbed up and pushed the wooden board up into the attic. Reaching up, she took a firm grasp on the edges, and with a jump and some creative wiggling, she managed to get her upper body through the hole. She collapsed onto the attic floor, pulled up her legs, and looked around.

To one side was a short passageway and a door to the roof. To the other side, the room opened up into the circular attic space above her tower room. The walls were short, only eighteen inches high, and then the roof leaned in all around up to the pointed roof. There was some light coming in from the window on one side of the tower roof, but it looked as if it hadn't been cleaned since it was first put in. She shined her light around, checking for anything hiding in the dim corners. The room was clear until a wall of boxes piled half-way across the room. Carefully, she walked around the boxes and over to the window. It pulled in, so she was able to get most of the dirt off. As she closed the window and turned, she thought she caught a glimpse of something moving near the boxes.

She hesitated, wishing that Amos was here. He was always willing to go investigate things like this for her. She took a breath and tiptoed across the floor. She looked over the pile of boxes and frowned. It looked like a small campsite set up behind the boxes. There were candle stubs set in the middle of the space, and the boxes were stacked to make different areas almost like rooms, some with throw pillows stuck in the corners of them. "It looks like a fort," she muttered. "Have they built a fort up here?"

Elise examined the attic one last time, looking carefully around to see if she had missed anything. She looked at her footprints in the dust and had a moment of regret that she hadn't looked for footprints before she walked around so much. The Leprechaun said they were passing through, but he might have lied. Elise shook her head. Could there really be Faerie creatures living in her attic? She thought of Uncle Jake's stories and of Kevan Foley's grin. Maybe there was.

She went back to the box fort and studied the layout. There was definitely a plan to this place. She could even see where they had set up a small kitchen. There were yogurt cups with flour and sugar, as well as one with coffee. It looked like the same things they had been taking last night. She counted the bedrooms. There seemed to be at least five beds, although it was hard to be sure. How many of them were there?

Elise heard a board creak behind her and whirled around. The attic was empty. She heard her aunt calling and went back to the trapdoor with a sigh. She would have to explore this place again and look to see if there was anything strange through the door to the roof.

As she came down from the attic, Amos sniffed her and growled. Elise rubbed his head. "Do I smell bad, Amos?" she asked. "Maybe I smell like Little People."

Amos trotted out the door and into the living room where Aunt Mim was waiting. "Did you find anything in your attic?" she asked.

"Just some boxes," Elise said. "They seemed to be arranged like a fort, but I didn't see anything living there."

"Maybe the last people had a son that built a box fort," said Aunt Mim absently. "As long as there are no mice nests or rats up there, I don't mind what else there is."

Back in her room, Elise sat in her rocking chair and thought about the mysterious fort in the attic.

"It's not what I expected, Amos," she said. "I don't think they are just passing through, but I don't know why they would want to live in our attic." Amos's tail thumped on the floor. "I know," Elise agreed. "We will have to figure this out."

* * * * *

Later that afternoon, Elise decided to go back into the attic and leave some food, hoping that would keep the Leprechaun and his friends from stealing food at night. She wasn't sure what food to choose, but remembering what she had seen, she took some coffee and some tea, along with a few crackers and some cheese. As an after-thought, she also added a chocolate bar. As a peace offering, choco-late seemed to be a pretty safe choice.

She poked her head up into the attic and looked around. More light was coming in from the newly-cleaned window, and she gasped at the rainbows floating around the attic. Elise wiggled through the hole and walked slowly to the window. Grams's prism hung from the window latch, rotating serenely. "How did you get here?" she asked, taking it from the latch and putting it in her pocket. She looked around and checked the fort, but there was still no sign of life. She placed the food in the middle of the floor and then let herself back down the trapdoor.

This was becoming more and more inexplicable. How could Grams's prism come to be hanging in the attic? Had Meallán and his friends stolen that too? The only way in was through the door on the roof or through her room. It didn't seem like they had any problems getting around, but she definitely didn't want them coming through her room at night. She stroked Amos's ears and hurried back to the living room. She had to solve this mystery soon, or she wouldn't get any sleep.

* * * * *

Elise stuck her head back into the attic the next morning and found the containers she had used stacked in a small pile near the edge. Inside the top one was a small green jewel. She took everything and sat on her bed to look at the jewel. Amos sniffed at it and gave the same small growl before lying back down. Elise looked at the jewel and frowned.

"I guess this solves it," she said to Amos. "It has to be that Leprechaun and his friends living in my attic. Who else would leave something like this in payment?"

Amos didn't really look interested but sniffed at the jewel again politely. After their meeting in the kitchen that night, he had seemed surprisingly unconcerned with the small invaders.

Elise and Amos went out for breakfast, and Elise took the prism. "Here Grams," she said as she handed it to her. "I found this."

"Where was it?" asked Grams in surprise. "I can't imagine how it came to be in with your stuff."

Elise shrugged and was thankful when Uncle Jake's arrival interrupted the conversation. They were going to work in the garden today to try to clean it up enough to make it useable.

"Has anyone seen my purple earrings?" Aunt Mim asked as she came out of her room. "I seem to have lost one of them."

"We all seem to have gotten careless or forgetful," said Grams. "Elise found my prism in with her things, but now I've lost one of my silver wind spinners. Maybe, in this big house, we are just finding more places to lose things."

Elise laughed along with everyone else, but she had the feeling the missing objects might turn up in the attic. Maybe the Little People were stealing more than food.

As they went out to work in the garden, Elise maneuvered Uncle Jake to where she was working at the side of the house. Far away from Aunt Mim. This wasn't a conversation that she wanted overheard.

"Uncle Jake," she began, "are the Little People good or bad?"

"Well, there are all kinds," he answered. "Some are good, and some are not so good. Most are neutral as far as humans are concerned. If you help them, they will be good to you, but if you hurt them or they feel threatened by you, they might try to do something to keep you away. Why?" he asked with a chuckle. "Did you find some Little People in your attic?"

"No, but there are some strange things that I can't explain and can't tell Aunt Mim."

Uncle Jake looked serious. "Well, be careful. In the stories, they are unpredictable at best, and you have to be very careful about what you say. Never promise to do something until you know what it is. And never tell them too much information. They are pretty tricky customers."

Elise nodded. That would be good to remember. "But how do you find them?" she asked.

"If they want to talk, they'll come to you," said Uncle Jake. "People who go to find them often end up with more trouble than they bargained for."

Elise sighed. This wasn't very helpful. Maybe she would just keep leaving food for them. At least then, they wouldn't have to go down to the kitchen and make Aunt Mim upset.

Uncle Jake occasionally compared Aunt Mim to a hurricane. Usually predictable, but she moved fast, and nothing could stop her once she got going. The upstairs guest rooms were nearly furnished. The downstairs kitchen had been remodeled in record time, and the inspectors had come and given their approval.

Once Aunt Mim got her tables delivered, the coffee shop could open. Grams, Aunt Mim, and Uncle Jake were busy planning a grand opening for the coffee shop and advertising for the bed-and-breakfast. The main argument was agreeing on a name, but finally, they reached an agreement, and Uncle Jake, who was in charge of the technical side of the advertising, launched the website for the Silverleaf Castle Bed & Breakfast and Castle Coffee. Aunt Mim looked proudly at the pictures that showed how much they had accomplished in the past few weeks.

"Now we have a deadline," she said. "We have to have every-thing ready in the next three weeks."

"That's her bossy voice," Uncle Jake whispered loudly to Elise. "That means she has lots of work for us to do."

Aunt Mim glared at Uncle Jake, but they both smiled. This day was too happy to even pretend to be annoyed with each other.

Every few nights, Elise had been leaving food in the attic. She didn't know how much the group needed, but she didn't want to make Grams and Aunt Mim suspicious, so it wasn't much. She left them some cereal, bread, more coffee, and sometimes, a few pieces of fruit or some cookies. Each time, the dishes were stacked neatly by the door, and there was another green stone left after the third time.

"There has to be a better way to do this," she complained to Amos. "People are going to start coming soon, and we can't have Leprechauns popping in and out of windows."

* * * * *

The next day, Elise decided to go up and have another look around. She stuck her head up into the attic and scanned the area. Nothing moved. She pulled herself up into the attic, this time remembering to look around for footprints. There were some scuffles in the dust but nothing clear. Something was living up here, but it wasn't leaving any clear signs. She went to the fort and looked inside. Nothing seemed to have changed. There were still the small pillows stuck around the rooms in the back, and the kitchen area with its rows of yogurt cups was still neatly arranged.

Suddenly, from behind her, she heard a cough. She turned slowly around and saw a small man standing just inside the door to the roof. Behind him, Elise could see another figure peering around the door. She looked back at the small man. He wasn't one that she had met that night in the kitchen. There *were* more of them. This man was just taller than her knee but was stocky and looked very strong. He wore dark-brown pants and a lighter-brown shirt with a green jacket over it. His hair and beard were reddish-brown, and his skin was a light nutty-brown. There was a sword strapped to his back and a dagger on his belt. He looked exactly like a picture of a soldier. A very tiny soldier.

"Greetings, human child," the man began, bowing slightly. "On behalf of Prince Rauri, I offer you welcome to our outpost in the human world."

Elise just stared. He stood still, looking at her, and Elise realized he was waiting for her to respond.

"Um, greetings," she replied, bowing awkwardly. "I am Elise Alexander." She stopped, unsure of what else to say.

Apparently, that was enough because the small man bowed again. "We thank you for your gifts and have decided that, perhaps, you could be of service to our troupe."

Elise remembered what Uncle Jake had said about promising help and chose her words carefully. "I'm not sure what I could possibly do," she said. "What do you need help with?"

The man smiled. "Perhaps I can introduce you to the rest of our troupe and tell you our story." He nodded to the figure waiting outside and gave a few whispered commands. Elise watched as a small woman came through the door and bowed. She was dressed in a similar fashion to the man but carried a short sword at her side and had a bow and a quiver of arrows slung over her shoulder. Her hair was short and brown, and she had it tucked under a green cap that matched her jacket. She went to the far end of the fort and climbed up to the top of the boxes. She was obviously another soldier. Elise smiled, but the woman ignored her.

The man stood by the door as if he was waiting for something. Soon, more small people came in from the roof. They were different from the two soldiers, and all different from each other. Elise glared as the Leprechaun sauntered in. His round face twinkled, and he winked at Elise as he bowed politely. Behind him, came a man and a woman, both with round, wrinkled faces and spindly arms and legs that seemed too long for their round bodies. They gave her a friendly smile as they made their way to the kitchen. The Fairy flew out of the passageway and landed on the top of the fort near Elise. He glared down at the first soldier.

"Let's get going. We've waited long enough."

The woman answered instead. "We wait for the prince." She said it quietly, but no one argued with her. The Fairy nodded once and sat down with his back to Elise.

After a moment, another figure appeared in the entrance. It was Tíreachán. He looked at Elise and then at the first man. "Shall I inform the prince?" he asked briefly.

"Has no one told him yet?" the Fairy complained. "We've been waiting for him."

"You've been waiting all of one minute," said the woman from the kitchen. "Have some patience."

"I don't want to be patient any longer. We've been stuck here far too long!" shouted the Fairy.

"Enough," said the first soldier. "No more chatting until the prince arrives. He will decide what we tell the human." He turned back to Tíreachán. "Yes, inform the prince at once." Tíreachán disappeared back through the door, and everyone waited in silence.

Elise shifted from one foot to the other, unsure what she should do. It sounded like they knew she had seen them, but she wasn't sure what the Leprechaun had told them. She glanced around to see what everyone else was doing.

Meallán looked at her, winked, and tipped his hat. She blinked as she realized that he was wearing one of Aunt Mim's purple amethyst earrings stuck in his hat.

"That's Aunt Mim's earring!" she exclaimed. "Were you the one who took Grams's prism? What else have your stolen?"

Meallán's bold smile faded as the female soldier jumped off the box and stalked over. "We told you to stop stealing things!" She held out her hand and looked pointedly at his hat. "This is how troupes get caught." She snatched the earring away muttering, "Leprechauns," and handed it to Elise.

Before Elise could say anything, Tíreachán reappeared and announced, "Prince Rauri!"

Elise looked to see what the others were doing, but they simply sat and watched. She hesitated but then bowed as another small man came through the doorway. He was the tallest yet, and he looked almost like Tíreachán but was much lighter. His skin was tanned, but his hair was almost blond, and his eyes were green. He stood a little bit straighter, and his face was more noble and less kind. He looked like the kid at school who knows everyone will do whatever he says. He smiled and gave a slight bow in return.

"Welcome, human child," he said. "I am Prince Rauri of the Elven kingdom—"

"You're an Elf?" Elise interrupted and then clapped her hand over her mouth. She didn't want to offend these people. As small as they were, she would feel safer if they weren't angry with her.

Prince Rauri smiled. "Perhaps some introductions are in order." He pointed at the soldiers. "This is Fergal, and the lady is Neala. They are Gnomes of the highest character and are skilled in all areas of warfare." He paused while the two Gnomes bowed. Elise nervously bowed in return. She did not remember Gnomes being especially warlike, but really, the only Gnomes she knew were garden statues.

The prince continued. "This red-haired fellow is Meallán, a Leprechaun." More bowing. "Our two camp Brownies are Branna and Turlach, and the Fairy is named Laisrén." After more bowing, Elise looked at Tíreachán, waiting for his introduction. The prince noticed her gaze and added, almost impatiently, "You know Tíreachán. He is a Gruagacha." Elise bowed and wondered at the surprised look Tíreachán gave her as he bowed in return.

"My name is Elise," she said, hoping they would stop calling her *human child*. It was slightly disconcerting to be referred to as *human*. She supposed, though, that in this company, it was the easiest way to identify her. "Fergal said that you needed my help? What help could I possibly give you?"

Prince Rauri motioned for everyone to sit down. Tíreachán brought the prince a small box and Rauri sat without looking at the man.

"We are a troupe of explorers sent by King Brian of the Faerie Realm to investigate a shift in one of our passageways to your realm," Prince Rauri began. "It is one little used and more remote than some. We were not aware it had been changed until a roving Gnome discovered the passage came here, to this strange land, instead of to its usual place. We came through for the first time about six months ago and, after considering the implications of entering this land, returned about two months ago. However, since that time, the stone that opened the passageway has been removed, and we cannot find another way home. We are trapped here."

"You came here through a stone?" Elise asked, confused. "How does that work."

"Magic," said Meallán with a grin. "And we didn't come through a stone, we came through the Faerie Ring."

"Aren't there any other passages?" asked Elise. "I thought there were many ways to get to the Faerie Realm."

"Not in this country," answered Prince Rauri. "All of our passages are in what you call the *old country*. This new land belongs to other creatures. The passages here lead to a very different realm from our own. Perhaps we could find the way back by passing from realm to realm, but that is a last resort." He shot a look at Neala as he spoke. She looked stubbornly back at him, and Elise wondered if Neala had wanted to try this way. She certainly seemed like she wouldn't be afraid of anything.

"But what do you need me for?" Elise asked. "I don't know anything about passages to the Faerie Realm."

"You can find the stone," said Rauri simply. "We can describe its appearance, and you can help us search for it. We cannot let ourselves be seen by any humans, so we are limited in the thoroughness of our search. Some of us have been seen already." He glared at Tíreachán, who ducked his head and frowned.

"How will I know this rock when I see it?" Elise asked. "I can't just go around bringing in rocks for you to look at."

"Turlach can draw it," offered Branna. "If you have a picture, it should be easy to find."

Turlach nodded, and everyone looked up at Elise. They seemed to think this would be easy, but if they hadn't found the stone yet, that meant it probably wasn't around the house or garden. Where else could it have gone? What if the last family had taken it with them? She might never be able to find it.

Elise considered what Uncle Jake had told her about promising to help. "If you can give me a picture, I will keep my eyes peeled for it—"

"Peeled eyes?" interrupted Laisrén. "What nonsense is that? Why would you peel your eyes?"

"No, not really peeled. I mean I will watch for it. I may not be able to *search* for it, but if I see it, I will tell you."

"So you won't help us," said Neala sharply. "We are trapped here in your world, and all you will do to help is watch where you are walking."

Everyone started arguing at once. The gentle Brownies and Tíreachán seemed to be sympathetic to her, but Neala, Laisrén, and Meallán all shouted them down. Fergal said nothing; he just watched

Prince Rauri and Neala carefully, as if he expected some trouble to erupt between them. Prince Rauri finally got everyone under control.

"The human child is not obligated to help us," he said. "We will simply have to take more risks searching the house and the town. If the big humans see us, we will deal with that problem when it happens."

"Wait," said Elise. "Aunt Mim can't see you. She is stressed enough trying to get everything ready to open. If she sees a bunch of Little People running around, she will have a breakdown."

Prince Rauri looked at her with a haughty expression. "That is a chance we will have to take. Anything could be happening back in our realm. We must return as soon as we can."

"All right," Elise agreed. "I will try to help you find your rock. But I'm just a kid, and I can't go too many places by myself. Anyway, if Aunt Mim gets suspicious, I won't be able to do anything at all."

Prince Rauri offered his hand, and Elise shook it. "We are grateful for your help, Elise."

Elise slid back into her room to find Turlach some paper and a pencil. She pulled out her favorite short pencil which her teacher had finally forbade her to use in class. It should be just the right size for Turlach.

"We were right, Amos," Elise said as she pulled out a notepad. "There are more of them and they are living in the attic. I'll tell you all about it. There's just one more thing I have to do." Amos whined as she went to climb back up into the attic.

"Sorry, buddy," Elise said. "I'll be back soon. Maybe we can figure out a way for them to come down. That way we can all talk together." She clambered back up into the attic and handed over the paper and pencil. "I need to go have lunch," she said. "Aunt Mim will come to see what's going on if I spend too much time in my room on such a nice day."

Prince Rauri nodded. "We will have the drawing ready for you when you return," he said. "In the meantime, look for any stone that seems out of place."

Elise nodded. She dropped back into her room and took Amos down to spend some time in the garden, just to ease any suspicions Grams or Aunt Mim might have. She usually didn't spend much time in her room during the day. Amos scouted the edges of the yard and gave a short baying bark near the shed. Elise recognized that bark and hurried over. Amos had found a scent. He growled and scratched at the stone foundation. There were some small footprints in the dirt.

"One of them must have come out here," she said to Amos as she smoothed out the dirt. "We can't let Grams or Aunt Mim see these tracks." She followed the tracks, smoothing out the dirt but stopped when they led into the shed.

"That's strange," she murmured, poking a stick at the hole in the corner. "I don't know why they would have gone inside and not come out." She motioned for Amos to follow her to the front of the shed. "I'll open the door, and you check it out. Maybe there are some other Little People stranded here." She flung open the door and flicked on the light. There didn't seem to be any sign of more Faerie, but before she could get Amos to go in, Aunt Mim called her in to eat.

"What have you been doing in your room all morning?" asked Grams.

"Just exploring the attic a bit more and sorting some things," Elise answered. "I have one more thing to do, and then I'm going to find something to do outside."

"You can find a nice flower bed," suggested Aunt Mim, "and take all the weeds out of it."

Elise smiled. "I could probably manage that," she agreed. She could help out and still take time to look around the garden. She was sure that the Gnomes would have found the stone if it was anywhere nearby, but it was all she could do today. Maybe tomorrow, when it was nice and bright, she could explore the basement. She hadn't gone down there much. The rooms were finished, but Aunt Mim was still deciding what to do with them. The bare walls and swinging light-bulbs made you feel like spiders were lurking in every corner.

Elise and Amos went back to her room after lunch, and Elise climbed back into the attic. To her surprise, Tíreachán was the only one there. He handed her the picture. "The others are all out doing reconnaissance," he explained. "I don't think they are really looking for the stone near the house anymore. We've looked so many times, but it's better than sitting here doing nothing."

"Do you often go out to the garden?" Elise asked. "Amos and I found tracks near the shed. They went in through that hole in the corner but not out. Are there any other people from your realm here?"

Tíreachán frowned and shook his head. "I don't think so," he said. "No one can come through if the stone is missing, and we would know if anyone had been around as long as we have. What did the tracks look like? I should tell Fergal."

Elise frowned. "I didn't want Aunt Mim to see them, so I wiped them out. Maybe we could find more somewhere in the garden. We didn't look anywhere else."

Tíreachán nodded. "I'll come with you. I'm not as good at tracking as the Gnomes, but I can probably tell what made them if they are clear enough. I'll meet you in the garden."

"How will you get there?" asked Elise.

"From the roof," said Tíreachán. "We can get anywhere from there without too much trouble." He smiled. "We can all climb the stonework here, and everyone else has magic that helps them get pretty much anywhere they want."

"Don't you have magic?" Elise asked. "I've never heard of Gru…" She stumbled to a stop.

"Gruagacha." Tíreachán prompted. "We are nearly the same as the Elves, but they claim we don't have magic. We have been the servants of the Elves for many generations." He stopped, and Elise thought he looked both sad and angry.

"Is that why everyone tells you what to do?" she asked cautiously. "They really aren't very nice."

Tíreachán shrugged. "They treat all Gruagacha like this. We have been trying for many years to regain an equal standing in the Faerie Realm, but without magic, they will always look down on us."

"That doesn't seem fair," said Elise. "Not everything can be solved by magic, so surely, there must be ways for you to show them you are just as smart or brave as they are."

Tíreachán smiled. "That is what my mother always told me. It is easy to forget what you can do when you always feel that you are somehow less than those around you. Thank you for the reminder."

Elise smiled and went back for Amos. She remembered the picture Tíreachán had given her and looked at it carefully. It was an amazingly detailed, if somewhat small, picture. She should definitely be able to recognize the stone if she saw it. It was roughly rectangular with smooth lines where it had been carved. Vines wrapped around the stone in an intricate pattern. The flowers were the same ones that were carved into the pillars of the house. There couldn't be too many stones like it.

Elise and Amos went down to the garden and looked around for Tíreachán. She was about to call for him when Aunt Mim stuck her head out the back door. "Which flower bed will you work on this afternoon?" she asked as a pointed reminder.

"I think one of the ones near the shed," Elise answered. "It could be a cute little building if it was cleaned up a bit."

"Those are mostly rose bushes," said Aunt Mim, "so make sure you wear thick gloves if you pull out any dead branches. Otherwise, just work on cleaning out the grass and shorter plants and then mulch around it." She smiled as she turned to go in. "Start on the side facing the house. We can always do the parts no one will see later."

"Sure," said Elise. "I'll just check out all around to see what we're up against."

Aunt Mim threw her a kiss as she went back inside, and Elise jogged off toward the shed. "Tíreach—" she called as loudly as she dared, tripping over his name.

He stuck his head out of the bushes behind the shed and motioned for her to come around the corner, out of sight from the house. "Call me Tír," he said. "It's much easier." He looked around the garden. "There are plenty of places to hide around here. I'll check around the shed for more tracks."

"I need to start working on the front," Elise said. "There aren't any tracks there anymore, so I can pull up all the grass and stuff so Aunt Mim doesn't come out to see what's going on."

Elise dug up the weeds from the back corner, near the hole in the shed. She had cleared nearly a foot from the end when Tír popped his head around the corner. He looked worried.

"I found some tracks, but they aren't very clear," he began. "At least, I hope they aren't what I think they are." He paused. "I need to go find one of the Gnomes or the prince. He's almost as good as the Gnomes at tracking," he said proudly.

Tíreachán ran off, and Elise kept tearing out the plants from around the rose bushes along the side of the shed. The roses got thicker as she went on, and after pricking her fingers on the thorny branches, she went to get some gloves from the shed. She opened the door but stumbled back as Amos bounded past her, barking.

"What's wrong, you crazy dog?" Elise demanded. The pile of tarps in the back corner crinkled as something ran through them. Amos charged into the pile after it. Elise shrieked and tried to pull him away. Amos finally gave up the search, and Elise managed to grab some gloves on her way out. She would wait for someone else to come before she investigated any further. She pulled out a few more plants before Amos sniffed his way around the edge of the shed and growled again at the corner where the hole was. Elise went over and saw the same tracks in the dirt, this time leading away from the shed. She pulled Amos away. "Leave the tracks alone," she warned. "When the Gnomes come, they will be able to tell what was in there."

Laisrén darted past and landed on one of the rose bushes. "Everyone is coming," he said, making a sour face. "Tíreachán made such a fuss that Neala made everyone come. I think she hopes he is wrong, so she can make him look bad in front of the prince."

"Why does she dislike him so much?" asked Elise.

"She dislikes almost everyone," said Laisrén. "She gets grumpier the longer we stay here. Prince Rauri won't let her go look for another way back. She thinks there is trouble at home, and we have been purposely stranded here." He smirked a little. "She is also impatient. She would rather take the chance of traveling through the wild realms than wait any longer. And if there is trouble at home, Tír might—" Whatever he was going to say about Tír was cut off when the rest of the company popped out of the flowers behind the shed.

"Where are these terrible tracks?" asked Neala sarcastically. Tíreachán pointed her to the other side, but Elise stopped him.

"I think Amos scared something out of the shed. It left really clear tracks just here." She pointed to the corner of the shed and watched in alarm as the entire troupe took one look and froze.

"Phookas!" muttered Neala. "How'd they get here?"

"It is just one," said Fergal. "Maybe it came over before the stone was removed and has just now returned to try to get back," he suggested. "There is no reason to assume it is here for any other purpose than trying to get home."

"What's a Phooka?" asked Elise. This was something she had never heard of before.

"Phookas are shapeshifters," answered Fergal. "In their true form, they are big. Much bigger than any of us, and they are not fond of Elves, or Gnomes, or anyone with them. In the Human Realm, they usually take the shape of black dogs or cats, or even rats sometimes, but their tracks don't change, which is how you can tell a Phooka from a real animal. When they change into other animals, they can change their size, which is how it can fit through that hole."

"But what is it doing here?" asked the prince, almost to himself. He looked at the tracks and then across the garden toward the Faerie Ring.

"It could have forced open the passage temporarily," said Laisrén. "If it had a few Pixies and enough Pixie dust, it could have gotten through."

"At least it's just one," said Branna. "All together, we must be more than a match for one Phooka."

Fergal nodded. "Yes, but it is still dangerous. We will have to take precautions." He looked sternly at Neala. "No one is to try to take on the Phooka alone." Neala made a face but did not respond.

"He is right," said Prince Rauri, focusing on the group again. "We cannot afford any injuries while we are unable to get back home. If something happens in this realm, you may not survive."

The Brownies nodded seriously, and Meallán laughed. "Don't worry. No one would be crazy enough to take on a Phooka alone." The others agreed. Neala smiled bitterly but still said nothing.

"What about me?" asked Elise. "Will it hurt me?"

"Not with that dog around," said Fergal. "He should be able to smell any Phooka long before it is close enough to attack. I'll just have a word with him and be sure he knows what to do."

"You can talk to him?" Elise gasped. "He talks to you? What does he say?"

"It isn't exactly talk like we do, but he understands well enough what's going on," replied Fergal. "Neala had a word with him after he caught Tír that night in the kitchen. He hasn't bothered about us since."

Elise looked at Amos in surprise. "You knew about all of them?" she asked. "Why didn't you tell me somehow?"

"Neala can be pretty convincing," Fergal said with a grin. Neala smiled sweetly but with a bite behind it. "Poor Amos was in a tough spot. Luckily, you found us yourself, so he didn't have to worry anymore."

Elise looked at Amos in disbelief. He wagged his tail and licked her hand. He had known about all of the Little People? He could talk? Maybe she would have to get Fergal to translate for them sometime. "Can anyone else talk to Amos?" she asked in a small voice. It would be awful if she was the only one left out.

Meallán laughed. "No. We can sometimes guess what he is saying, but no one really understands animals except the Gnomes. It gives them a great advantage in the forest. That and talking with the plants," he added slyly.

Elise blinked. This was getting to be too much. Neala smirked and went over to the rose bush next to the tracks. She started whispering and then crouched down near the base of the plant.

"Now she's just showing off," grumbled Laisrén.

Neala's smirk vanished suddenly, and she whispered urgently to the rose bush. After a moment, she came back and shook her head. "It's more serious than we thought," she said. "According to the rose, the Phooka has a scar across its face." She paused to let her words sink in. "There is only one Phooka I know of with a scar like that."

"Baoth," said Rauri grimly. "This cannot be a coincidence. Either he was sent here after us before the stone was removed, or someone forced him through afterward to keep us from coming back. Either way, we need to find the stone quickly and get back to the Faerie Realm. If Baoth is here, then Murtagh must be back."

The rest of the company was silent. Not even Laisrén made a joke. Tíreachán frowned and muttered something under his breath. Neala glared at him suspiciously but didn't say anything.

"We have to find the stone," Prince Rauri said again. "I fear that there is grave trouble in our realm."

Elise hurried to finish weeding while the Little People discussed this new development. After a few minutes, the Brownies came over to help.

"They are talking about what-ifs and strategies and don't need our help with that," Branna said cheerfully. "Flowers are much more peaceful and pleasant to be around." Elise smiled at the funny little creatures. Their faces were wrinkly, but neither Turlach nor Branna seemed very old. Their round bodies and skinny arms and legs made them look a little bit like spiders, with hands and feet too big for their skinny limbs. They had kind smiles, though, and their serene personalities calmed the group when others got excited.

Turlach reached into the bag he wore slung over his shoulder and pulled out a small trowel, which he handed to Branna.

"You always have a tool for any job," she said with a fond smile.

Branna stuck the small trowel in the ground, and Elise's jaw dropped as a clump of grass taller than the Brownie fell over, roots and all.

"It's magic," Turlach explained with a smile. "We Brownies don't do magic, but we can make any object magic." He patted the bag at his side. "It does make life much easier to have a few things ready for emergencies."

"Weeding a flower bed was an emergency you thought of?" Elise asked. "Aunt Mim would love you. We have a whole garden to get through!"

"You should get Tír to help," said Branna. "He comes from a long line of farmers and knows his way around plants."

Elise frowned, suddenly remembering what Fergal had said about that night in the kitchen. She had been too distracted by the fact that Amos could talk to ask about it. "What did Fergal mean about Amos catching Tír in the kitchen?"

The Brownies glanced at each other before Branna answered. "Meallán said Tír was too noisy in the kitchen, and Amos heard him. Meallán was able to turn invisible, but Tír was caught. That's how you found out about us. Amos started looking for more of us after that, so Neala found him before he could give us all away."

Elise frowned. "That's not what happened. I heard Meallán and Laisrén talking and turned on the light. I saw them all. Amos caught Meallán. Why didn't Tír explain what happened?"

Branna frowned. "He probably thought no one would believe him." She looked at Turlach. "We didn't even think to question Meallán, although he *is* one of those Leprechauns who doesn't always worry too much about the right way of things."

"Well, he lied about Tír," said Elise, firmly defending her new friend. "I'll even tell the prince if I have to." Elise stopped as Tír stalked over.

"The prince has ordered me to help you," he said, frowning at the weeds. "He wants to get started looking for this Phooka as soon as possible."

"Can he just order everyone around like that?" Elise asked.

Tír gave a short laugh. "Technically, yes, since he's the prince, but he usually asks everyone else."

"So you're his servant?" Elise asked.

Tíreachán looked at Branna and Turlach. "I see you've been learning about our realm," he said. "Let me explain from our point of view. Gruagacha are Elves, the same as the prince. Many generations ago, which is a great long time considering how long we all live, one of the kings became greedy for more power. He claimed that some Elf clans, including mine, were incapable of properly using magic, though we remember it differently. He made it illegal to teach the two smallest clans the ancient language and forced them to become farmers and laborers, creating a whole group of Elves who had very little power. They called us Gruagacha which, ironically, is the ancient word for peasant. It is one of the few ancient words we know well. We have served the high Elves ever since. We believe, though, that if the Gruagacha can learn the ancient language, then we can learn to do magic again, and the Elves will have to grant us our freedom, just like everyone else."

Elise stopped weeding and looked at him. "Then why do you serve the prince if you don't like the Elves?"

Tíreachán shuffled his feet and looked embarrassed. "He's actually a good prince," he admitted. "I don't have anything against him specifically, although he does tend to be a bit stuffy at times. He can't help that he's grown up thinking this way. They all do. Even the other peoples of our realm think we are inferior." He glanced at Branna and Turlach, who focused on the weeds they were pulling and pretended not to hear. "But as you reminded me, we have to try our best to prove that we are equal, with or without magic. I'm learning a lot from serving Prince Rauri. Maybe one day, I will have the chance to prove that the Gruagacha are not what everyone thinks we are."

"Who is Murtagh?" asked Elise. "Everyone seems worried about him."

"He is a powerful Elf magician. No one really knows where he came from, but many years ago, Murtagh tried to overthrow King Brian," Tír explained. "He promised that he would teach the Gruagacha the ancient language and set them free from serving the Elves. Many Gruagacha followed him, hoping that he would make things change. After he was defeated, he was banished with everyone who followed him. If he is back, then there is going to be trouble in the Faerie Realm."

They finished pulling up the last weeds from the rose garden. The dirt was fresh and dark under the prickly stems. The rose bushes were a bit wild, but the flower bed looked much better.

"Have you finished?" Prince Rauri asked, a bit impatiently.

"Not quite," answered Elise. "I have to put mulch over the dirt, or the weeds will just grow again. It will only take a few minutes, especially since it's right near the shed!" She grabbed a bucket and scooped out the mulch from the huge bag in the shed. As she dumped bucket after bucket near the roses, Tír, Branna, Turlach, and Meallán helped spread it around. Laisrén watched from his perch on the rose bush, and the Gnomes and Prince Rauri held a whispered meeting at the corner of the shed.

"Meet back in the attic," Prince Rauri told the others. "We have a lot to discuss."

As Elise walked back in, Aunt Mim looked up from her work in the big kitchen. "Finished already? And you remembered the mulch? And didn't just dump it over top of the weeds?"

"Of course not," said Elise. "It just didn't take as much time as I thought it would. The roses were so thick, there wasn't much growing around them anyway."

Aunt Mim looked out the window. "It does look good from here," she agreed, putting her arm around Elise's shoulders. "We should be able to open the coffee shop soon. There are tables and chairs coming from Kevan Foley's shop today, and the final paperwork from the state should come through sometime this week. Hopefully, our mouse problem doesn't come back before then. I haven't noticed any mess for a while, and there doesn't seem to be any food missing, so I think that's taken care of."

"Yes, I think it is," said Elise hastily. "Anyway, I'll just grab a snack and go clean up." She ran upstairs and grabbed some fruit and pack of crackers before going to her room. The Little People were waiting for her in her room.

"Amos has expressed his displeasure that you spend so much time in the attic where he can't hear what is happening," Fergal explained. "We have decided to hold our meetings down here in the future, since it is important that Amos knows how to protect you."

Elise looked at Amos, who lay smugly on his pillow near her bed. "Uh, that's great," Elise said. "I've brought some food in case anyone is hungry." She set the food on her desk and watched as Branna and Turlach went to divide it up. Since they told her about Tíreachán's role as a Gruagacha servant, she had realized that there were very different roles for each person based on their race. Brownies, it seemed, were in charge of the kitchen and the food. She would have to talk to them to make sure Meallán didn't start making a mess again.

"We have been talking," Prince Rauri said to Elise, "and we believe that the stone is not anywhere near the house. We have been looking carefully for weeks and have seen no trace of it. We believe, then, that someone must have taken it from the garden between the time we left on our exploration of this realm and the time we came back. We have to find this person and get it back."

"That could be anyone," began Elise. "The house was empty for months, and anyone could have come into the garden."

"That is true," agreed the prince, "but who would take that specific rock?"

Elise went to her desk and found the drawing that Turlach had made. The rock was interesting but not beautiful. Who would want a stone from this house?

From downstairs, Elise heard the doorbell ring. She glanced out her window and saw a truck full of tables and chairs. "Mr. Foley!" she shouted.

"Who?" demanded Neala.

"Kevan Foley," she exclaimed. "His great-great-grandfather or something built this house. Mr. Foley just came back from Ireland a few months ago to sell the house. He must have taken the stone as a keepsake since it belonged to his family."

"It makes sense," said Meallán. "If the stone came from Ireland that would explain what happened with the passageway. The opening on this end had changed."

"We have to hurry," said the prince. "Maybe we can find the stone if we can follow this Kevan Foley home."

"You'll have to hide in his truck," said Elise. "It will go too fast for you to follow. But I know where his shop is, and I bet I can find out where he lives, too. Then we can just go there together."

Prince Rauri thought for a moment before issuing crisp orders. "Laisrén, hide in the truck and begin the search. We will join you as soon as we can. Now that there is a Phooka on the loose, we should limit our use of magic to necessity only. We do not want to be any easier to find than we have to be."

Laisrén nodded and flew to the window. "Mind giving me a hand?" he asked Elise, pointing to the screen. She lifted it up, and he flew toward the truck.

Prince Rauri continued. "Fergal and Neala, we will use the passageways and try to listen to what he is saying. See if there is any indication that he has the stone. Everyone else, back to camp and wait. We do not want too much noise."

The Brownies and Meallán nodded, but Tíreachán looked stubborn.

"I can be as quiet as anyone," he said.

Prince Rauri looked surprised at this minor rebellion but shook his head. "We three are enough," he said as he and the Gnomes slipped out the door. There were, apparently, other ways to get around the house unseen than going over the roof.

Elise decided that since the prince hadn't given her any instructions, she would go talk to Mr. Foley and see what she could find out. She called to Amos and went downstairs. Mr. Foley and Aunt Mim were carrying chairs into the main rooms and arguing cheerfully about where they might look best.

"There you are," said Aunt Mim. "You can start matching the chairs to the tables as we bring them in." She pointed to the row of mismatched chairs against the wall. Tables of all different designs and colors were stacked in the truck. This was better than Christmas for Aunt Mim. Elise started matching chairs with tables until Aunt Mim and Mr. Foley finally brought in the last table.

"Thank you for delivering them," Aunt Mim said to Kevan. "Can I offer you a drink before you go?"

Kevan smiled. "Trying to get rid of me so you can place them any which way?" he asked with a smile. "All part of the delivery process is helping the poor buyer know just where to put each one."

Aunt Mim smiled, and Elise rolled her eyes. She may not be able to ask too many questions if they were going to be talking like this.

Aunt Mim showed Kevan the rooms that they were going to use for the coffee shop. She also took him outside to show him her ideas for outdoor seating. Elise followed. This might be her chance to ask about the stone. As she and Amos walked out the back door, Amos growled and ran toward the shed, knocking Aunt Mim into Kevan.

"What has gotten into that crazy dog?" demanded Aunt Mim. "What does he think is in that shed?"

Amos was sniffing around the hole that the Phooka used.

"It could be anything," offered Kevan. "There are lots of animals in these woods." He looked around the garden fondly. "I spent a lot of time out here in my youth," he said. "I loved playing in these gardens and woods."

"It is lovely," agreed Aunt Mim. "My mother and Elise have enjoyed working to get the garden back into shape." She smiled at Elise who laughed.

"Yes, I love weeding gardens," she said drily. "But Mr. Foley, there is a place near the back that is really nice. Uncle Jake says it is a Faerie Ring, but one stone seems to be missing."

"Aye," said Kevan. "My great-great-grandfather brought those stones from Ireland. He said they had been in his family garden for centuries, and he wasn't going to leave them behind. Most of them are just plain stones, but there was one carved stone there that my mother dearly loved. She always said it was a Faerie Stone." He stopped and smiled fondly. "It was one of the few things I really wanted from this house."

Elise nearly jumped for joy. He had the stone! But it sounded like it wasn't something he was going to let go of easily. If it meant that much to him, how was she going to get it from him?

Aunt Mim led them back into the house, and Elise helped arrange the tables and chairs. It took much longer than she thought necessary because Aunt Mim and Kevan kept changing their minds and arguing about where to place each table. Finally, they finished, and she raced back to her room. Amos had gone up long ago. She found all the Little People gathered in her room.

"Amos has told us what you discovered," said Fergal. Elise shot Amos a dirty look, but he just wagged his tail happily, though Elise thought he looked a little smug. After finding out that he could talk, she wasn't too surprised to find out he was like this. It was how she imagined having a younger brother might be.

"Before we can make a plan," Prince Rauri began, "we have to locate the stone. Now that we know where to look, it should be easy. If you can go to the shop tomorrow, Neala will follow you and find out where it is. Perhaps Laisrén will have already located the stone by that time, and we can just go that night and get it."

"It might be in his house, though," Elise argued. "We know he has it, but we don't know where."

"We will eliminate the shop first, since that is the easiest place to look," said Fergal. "Hopefully, it will be there, and we can get it back to the house."

"How will you carry it?" asked Elise. "Isn't it big?"

"We will manage," said Neala. "Don't underestimate us because we are small in your world. We have a few tricks you have not yet seen."

Prince Rauri looked at Elise. "You could come with us," he suggested. "It is true that we could get it back to the house, but it would take considerable effort and the risks of being seen are quite high."

Amos growled and gave a low bark.

"He said your aunt would not like it," said Fergal. "And that you are afraid of going out in the dark."

Neala snorted and remarked, "We don't need her help. She would just get in the way and probably get us caught."

Prince Rauri shook his head. "It is a risk, but it would be a help," he admitted. "Then, we will not have to use so much magic to move the stone. It will be difficult moving something that large over a long distance, and if there is a Phooka on the loose, we may need to fight."

"I'm not sure..." began Elise, stopping to look at Neala. "I think I can't go with you. I would have to sneak out, and if anyone saw me, I'd be in big trouble. I'm sorry. I can help you find the stone, but I can't help you take it."

Prince Rauri nodded. "We understand. Once you locate the stone, we will find a way to get it back here."

A knock on the door interrupted the prince, and the whole troupe vanished under or behind various pieces of furniture as Grams stuck her head in the door. "Dinner is ready," she said, looking around the room. "It looks nice in here. How do you like your tower?"

Elise swallowed and laughed nervously. "It's great!" she exclaimed. "I'll be right out for dinner." She hurried to wash her hands and get ready. She hoped the Little People found the stone soon and were able to go back home. They were making her life much more interesting than she would like.

* * * * *

Elise woke in the middle of the night to Amos jumping on her. "Get off," she said grumpily. "Stay on your end of the bed," she added as she pushed him toward the foot of the bed. Amos ignored her and licked her face. He ran to the door and whined.

Elise sighed and sat up. "You know that going out in the middle of the night means going all the way downstairs," she grumbled. "What's wrong with you anyway? You never have to go out at night." Amos was adamant, however, and Elise finally put on her slippers and opened the door.

They walked softly downstairs, and Elise opened the back door. Amos ran out but then stopped and ran back to her. He nudged her hand and ran back to the edge of the porch, clearly waiting for her. Elise turned on all the lights and grabbed a flashlight. "You know it's really dark out here," she squeaked as she followed him. "This had better be important."

They hadn't gone far when they met Branna running up the path. "You're here!" she exclaimed. "We hoped Amos would hear us calling for him, but we had just given up." She hurried through the grass and led Elise and Amos to a hidden corner of the garden. "Fergal has been hurt, and we weren't sure how to get him up into the house. We can't climb while carrying him, and we weren't sure we could risk carrying him up all the stairs out in plain sight." Elise stopped short at the sight of Fergal lying still in the grass. Turlach was wrapping a piece of cloth around his head while Neala tied a bandage around his side. Tíreachán sat quietly while Meallán wrapped a bandage around his arm.

"What happened?" Elise asked.

"Baoth," replied Neala shortly. "The prince is checking to be sure he is gone, but we will need some help getting Fergal back upstairs."

Elise nodded and tried to calm her breathing. She sat down in the grass and took a few deep breaths. "Okay," she whispered to herself. "Everything is okay." She waited a moment until she felt less shaky and then looked up to find the Little People all looking at her with concern.

"Are you all right?" Branna asked kindly.

"Yes," said Elise, looking at Fergal. He needed help, and she was the only one who could do it. "Let's go," she said as she carefully lifted him.

She carried Fergal upstairs, turning the lights off behind her. The others elected to go up their own way, which was lucky because, just as Elise got into her room, she heard Aunt Mim's voice.

"Is everything all right, Elise?" she asked, sticking her head out of her bedroom door.

Elise stuck her head back around the corner, careful to keep Fergal hidden behind the doorway. "Fine," she replied. "Amos just decided he needed to go out. I think he forgot how far down it was."

"Okay," her aunt said with a yawn. "Good night."

"Good night," Elise responded, ducking back through the doorway.

When she got into her room, everyone was there waiting for her. She put Fergal down carefully on the pallet someone had made on the floor and watched with concern as Branna and Turlach fussed over him.

"What happened?" she asked again. "How did he get hurt?"

"He was out making one last round before turning in for the night," began the prince. "Neala and Tír were out with him. We have not heard the whole story ourselves yet," he added looking at Neala.

"I heard a noise in the bushes and went to investigate," Neala began. "I thought it was just some animal, but it was Baoth. Fergal must have guessed that because he jumped in front of me just as Baoth attacked. Baoth's claws caught him in the side, and when he fell, his head must have hit a rock. I fought Baoth off while Tír pulled Fergal out of the way." She looked at the Gruagacha with some respect. "He hadn't even pulled his sword, but he went charging in and got Fergal out. Baoth got him on the arm but then ran off when he lost the element of surprise."

"It's just a scratch," Tír said nervously when everyone looked at him. "I really didn't do much."

"You saved his life," Neala said fiercely.

"For now," Branna said. Everyone looked at her with surprise. "Phooka wounds are tricky," she explained. "Wounds are harder to heal anyway in the Human Realm, and he is hurt very badly. We need to get him home as soon as possible."

"Can't you do magic?" Elise asked.

"No one has that kind of strong magic," explained Branna. "Some Elves can use their magic to heal, but it is more for controlling the energy in the air and water around them. Leprechauns mostly just turn invisible but can do a bit of fire magic when needed. Gnomes can talk to plants and animals and be so still that people think they are statues. Brownies have their magical objects. Fairies can do lots of different magic, but their power is limited in the Human Realm and not very useful for healing anything. We have some magic medicinal objects that will help the wound from the Phooka but nothing for a head wound this serious."

"We have to find the stone," Rauri said, "and go home tomorrow night. Fergal cannot wait any longer than that."

"I can go to the shop tomorrow," offered Elise. "If the stone is there, Laisrén should have found it, and we can make a plan. If not, it will have to be at Mr. Foley's house, and we will have to figure out how to get in there." Elise stopped. She couldn't believe that she was really planning to do this. She looked at Fergal, pale in the dim light from her lamp. He had to get home quickly.

The next morning, Elise was awake early, despite her short night. Branna was sitting beside Fergal. "How is he?" Elise asked.

"A slight fever," Branna said softly. "His wounds are clean, but he hasn't woken up yet. If he doesn't wake up soon, there could be real danger." She felt his forehead. "He needs to get back to the Faerie Realm as soon as he can."

Elise went out and poured herself some cereal. She would have to plan this carefully. She needed to get into Mr. Foley's store on her own but couldn't think of a reason to go to town by herself. After all the times she had refused to go places alone, Aunt Mim and Grams would be shocked if she suggested it. She didn't like going places alone. She took her cereal back to her room. The shop wouldn't be open for a few more hours. She would talk to Prince Rauri and make a plan.

The others began to trickle in as she ate breakfast. They all pretended that they had something else to do in Elise's room, but their main concern was Fergal. Prince Rauri and Neala were the last to come. They had been out early searching for any sign of Baoth.

"Any change?" Neala asked, her hands nervously adjusting Fergal's blanket and pillow, before she forced herself to be still. Elise had never seen her show this much emotion about anything before.

Branna shook her head. "He isn't waking up. He needs to get back to the Faerie Realm as soon as possible. We are using all the magic we have, but it's just not enough."

Prince Rauri nodded and motioned for everyone to listen. "We need to find the stone as soon as possible," he began.

"I can go to Mr. Foley's store as soon as it opens," Elise interrupted. "But we will have to wait for tonight to get the stone." She hesitated for a moment. "Unless we just ask to borrow it," she finished, looking at Prince Rauri.

He considered for a moment but then shook his head. "It is unlikely that he will believe you. It is also very dangerous for us to show ourselves to adult humans. There are terrible stories of what humans have done to any of our people they have managed to capture. It will just make him suspicious and hurt our chances of getting the stone." He looked at Fergal. "We will have to wait and take the chance tonight."

Elise nodded but was disappointed. Asking would have been much easier, and she was sure that Mr. Foley would believe her. But she could understand how Prince Rauri would be afraid of other humans. They probably would have people doing experiments on them if they were caught.

* * * * *

The whole troupe fidgeted around Elise's room until she decided it was time to go. She found Aunt Mim busily cleaning the new tables and chairs and arranging decorations around the rooms. It was really starting to look like a coffee shop.

"May I walk into town?" Elise began. "I want to see if I can find the library and maybe stop one or two other places." She didn't want to lie to Aunt Mim, but she couldn't explain in detail either. Finding the library would be nice anyway; she would need some books to keep her busy after all the Little People left.

Aunt Mim smiled. "On your own? That's great!" She laughed and added, "One or two places? Like the Cree-Mee?"

Elise pretended to be surprised. "I never thought of that! I could get some ice cream!" This would make everything easier.

"The three identical musketeers," Aunt Mim said. "Yes, you may go. Just pay attention to the time and don't eat too much ice cream too close to lunch. Make sure you have your phone, and if you get into any trouble, call."

Elise smiled and walked out the door. She hesitated on the front porch and took a breath. Although she had been to town several times with Aunt Mim and Grams, this would be the first time ever that she had walked somewhere on her own. She took Amos's leash and walked to the road. She could see the sign for the Cree-Mee just at the bend and knew that town was just beyond that. She took three deep breaths and made a mental plan for her trip. Instead of searching for the library, she decided to go to Kevan's shop and just ask him where it was. That would give her a good reason to stop by, and she could look around for a bit, just for good measure. She would stick to the plan, and everything would be fine. She would find the stone and help save Fergal.

Elise took one last look at the house and caught Aunt Mim watching her from the window. She blew her a kiss as Aunt Mim waved cheerfully. *The first few steps will be the hardest*, she told herself. *Once you get going it will be easy. Just pretend Grams is walking behind, the way she always does.*

With these thoughts firmly in her mind, Elise made it to the Cree-Mee at the bend in the road. She could see town clearly now and, looking back, she could see the front yard of the house. She took a few more deep breaths and turned resolutely back toward town. She could do this.

She went straight to Mr. Foley's shop and felt a surge of relief as the bell jangled. Amos waited outside. He was used to waiting for her. Mr. Foley stuck his head around a pile of stuff.

"You can bring that hound of yours in as long as he doesn't make a mess," he said. "No need for him to sit outside and scare people away."

Elise opened the door and called Amos in. He walked over and sniffed Mr. Foley's shoes politely. "He says thanks," Elise said.

Mr. Foley smiled. "What can I do for you?"

"I was actually going to look for the library, but I thought I'd see if you knew where it was," Elise said.

"Always happy to help a fellow bibliophile," said Mr. Foley.

"A what?"

"Bookworm," he said with a laugh. "Someone who loves books." He gave her directions to the library, which was not too far away. Elise thought for a moment. She hadn't had time to look around yet.

"I was also thinking of buying something for Aunt Mim," she said, suddenly realizing it was a good idea. "She has been working really hard, and I want to get her something for when the coffee shop opens."

Mr. Foley beamed. "Fabulous idea! What did you have in mind?"

"I don't know," said Elise honestly. "Can I just look around and see what I find?"

"Of course," said Mr. Foley. "I'll be around or in the back. Just give a shout if you need anything."

Elise smiled and started to walk around the shop. There were lots of things Aunt Mim would love. She only had a few dollars in her pocket, however, so she would have to come back. Perfect if she didn't find the stone right now.

Amos had wandered away and was sniffing around near the counter. Suddenly, Elise saw the perfect thing. It was a crystal paperweight in the same shape as the carvings on the walls of the entryway and on the stone. The leaves looked suspiciously like the green stone that had been left in the food dishes, and the flower's five petals were a brilliant red. She picked it up carefully. It was more money than she had, but she could convince Grams to go in with her.

"Mr. Foley?" she called.

"Come on back," he called through the doorway behind the counter. "And please, call me Kevan," he added as she came through. He looked at the paperweight. "That is perfect," he agreed. "It was my great-great-great-grandfather's, and he claimed that the crystals came from the Faerie Realm. My great-great-great-grandmother said they were just glass, and he had them made so he could tell lies about being friends with the Faerie." He laughed. "There is a bit of crazy back many generations in my family."

"It's the same flowers that are carved in the pillars in the entry-way of the house," Elise said.

"They are. My family has been using those flowers to decorate for a long while," Kevan said.

"I don't have enough money with me today," she confessed. "But I can bring the rest tomorrow."

"That'll be fine," he said as he started wrapping the paperweight. "You can take it with you today and pay me later. Anyway, if you don't, I know where to find you." He smiled and handed it back to Elise. Just then, the bell jangled again. "Be right back," Kevan said as he jumped up.

Elise glanced around the back room. Amos was sniffing around the other end of the long desk and suddenly gave a short bark.

A sharp voice came from behind a vase on the shelf. "Quiet, you dumb dog. He'll hear you!" Laisrén stuck his head out and glared at them both. "It's here somewhere," he continued. "I can feel it. We went straight back to his house yesterday, and he's been in here all morning, so I haven't been able to look for it too much."

Amos growled and put his front legs up on Kevan's chair. Suddenly, Elise saw what he was trying to tell her. The stone was on Kevan's desk. It was right below the shelf so Laisrén couldn't have seen it from his position above. She pointed at it without saying anything.

"Figures," Laisrén muttered, fluttering upside down to look at the stone. "I've spent the past two hours staring around the room, and it was right under me the whole time."

Elise smiled. "Well, you can come back with me if you want," she said. "Everyone else is coming tonight to get the stone." Suddenly, she gasped. Laisrén hadn't heard about Fergal. Quickly, she told him what had happened and why it was more important than ever that they get the stone quickly.

"That's bad," Laisrén agreed. "I'll wait here, though. It will be helpful to have a man on the inside if we are breaking in. Tell the prince I'll be ready and will try to find them an easy way in. Send Neala to investigate both doors before they do anything stupid and break something."

Elise nodded. She probably wouldn't say that exactly, but Laisrén was right. He could be very helpful and would have plenty of time to explore after Kevan went home.

She and Amos went out through the shop and said goodbye to Kevan. Elise decided that she might as well go to the library. If everything went according to plan, she might even have time to read tomorrow.

Elise found the library and met the librarian, who knew Uncle Jake and was delighted to help Elise get a library card and show her around. After choosing a few books, she stopped at the Cree-Mee to celebrate her morning's work.

Aunt Mim was waiting when she got back, and Elise told her about the library and stopping at Kevan's shop for directions. She made Amos stay with her, so he didn't go and tell the Little People first. Aunt Mim beamed with pleasure, and Elise felt a pang of guilt. She escaped upstairs to drop off her bag and tell everyone about finding the stone. As she and Amos burst into the room, everyone scattered but quickly came back out when they saw it was Elise.

"We found it!" she exclaimed as they all gathered around. "It's in the back room of Kevan's shop. Laisrén said he would stay and try to find a way for everyone to get in. He said to make sure you checked both doors before you tried to go in," she added, looking at Neala.

She smiled grimly. "I doubt he said it quite so politely." She turned to Prince Rauri. "If we have someone on the inside, everything should go smoothly."

Everyone paused for a moment, uncertain what to say. They had been waiting so long for this moment, but there were still many things that could go wrong. Fergal didn't have time for them to make any mistakes.

* * * * *

After dinner, Elise helped clean up and went to her room as soon as she could get away. She packed her backpack with a few things she might need: a flashlight, a jacket, and a hat in addition to the things that were always in there. She had a water bottle, some food, her phone, a small first-aid kit, and a Swiss Army knife that Uncle Jake had given her for her birthday last year. She loved all the little tools that it had; it made her feel prepared for anything, although sneaking out at night to break into someone's store was not a scenario that had occurred to her before.

Elise sighed as she got ready for bed. She would need to sleep early so she was ready to go out with the Faerie troupe. At first, her mind was too busy imagining Aunt Mim catching her sneaking out with the troupe of Little People to let her sleep, but finally, the excitement of the day caught up with her, and she dozed off. She woke up to Amos licking her face. It was time to go.

The house was dark, and Elise felt the familiar feeling of panic creeping up her throat. She was going outside in the dark and walking to town. She was doing something Aunt Mim wouldn't like. She stopped for a minute to catch her breath. She looked at Fergal's pale face in the lamp light and Branna's worried frown as she watched over him.

"Are you okay?" Tíreachán asked quietly. "If you can't go, we will find another way," he continued.

Elise shook her head. "I want to help Fergal," she said. "I won't be out alone, and I'm probably as safe with you all as I am with Aunt Mim."

Tír smiled. "With Prince Rauri and Neala with us, we have nothing to worry about!" he exclaimed.

Neala gave him a sour look and motioned for them to hurry. The Little People were ready to go. Elise threw on her sweatshirt and grabbed her backpack. She and Amos slipped out of her room and down the stairs without anyone hearing. Outside, she met up with the troupe, who had climbed down from the roof. They set off down the driveway. Elise was surprised at how fast they could go. She had to walk very quickly to keep up.

It was much darker than Elise had expected. She took out her flashlight, but Neala stopped her.

"We can't let people see us," she whispered fiercely. "There is enough light from the moon to see."

Elise swallowed and nodded, though she thought that there wasn't enough light for anyone to see even that. She had taken a few more steps when she felt something brush her hand. She jumped and let out a little squeak. "Shh!" Neala scolded sharply.

"It's just me," whispered Tíreachán. "I'll walk with you." He reached up and took her hand. Elise gripped it tightly as they kept moving toward town.

She led them to Kevan's store and waited while Neala went to check things out. This was the most dangerous part for her. If anyone saw her out alone at this time of night, they would be very suspicious. Neala came back and led them to the back of the building where Laisrén had simply unlocked one of the windows. Elise looked surprised, remembering how he had asked for help with her screen. "Since there wasn't anyone around, he just used magic," Meallán explained.

Elise opened the window and gave the prince and Neala a boost into the shop. Meallán and Turlach climbed onto the window frame and waited. Tír stood at the end of the alley and kept watch. Elise wanted to ask how they would get the stone out, but everyone seemed too busy. Soon, the stone appeared, hovering near the open window, and Meallán and Turlach grabbed it and pulled it through. It fell on the other side with a thump. Prince Rauri and Neala climbed out the window, followed by Laisrén, who motioned to Elise to close it behind them. They all stood looking at the stone with amazement. Laisrén was the first to break the silence. "Let's stop staring at it and go home," he said grumpily. "I've spent all day in that shop, and I'm hungry."

His complaint broke the spell. Elise picked up the stone. It wasn't very heavy, but she was pretty sure she would get tired of carrying it before they got back. Prince Rauri sent Tíreachán and Meallán back to gather their belongings from the camp and make sure Branna and Fergal were ready to go. Elise would drop the stone at the circle and then go get Fergal. The two ran ahead and disappeared.

They snuck out of town but relaxed as they passed the Cree-Mee. "How did you get the stone out?" asked Elise.

"Magic," explained Prince Rauri. "It took a lot of energy here, but I made it float just long enough to get it out the window."

"Magic doesn't work as well in your realm as it does in ours," complained Laisrén. "Nothing works as well as it should. That's why we depend mostly on being small and quiet in your world."

They walked straight to the stone circle. By the time Elise got there, she was more than happy to put the stone down. Prince Rauri showed her exactly where it should go. As soon as she placed it in the empty space, there was a small glow of light around the circle. It glowed for a few seconds and then faded. The Little People cheered but were quickly hushed by Neala.

Amos growled, and they all froze. Tír came out of the bushes. "Branna is ready for you to get Fergal," he said to Elise. "I'll walk back with you," he offered as she hesitated.

Elise nodded and smiled as he took her hand again. It was much easier walking through the dark with a friend. They crept upstairs, and Elise carefully picked up Fergal. Branna, Tír, and Meallán gathered the rest of their bundles and followed her back downstairs. They all crept outside and hurried back to the Faerie Ring.

Elise laid Fergal gently on the ground and turned to say goodbye to the troupe.

"This is where we take our leave of you," Prince Rauri said. "We thank you for your help and would like to offer you this gift to show our appreciation."

As he reached for his pack, Neala grabbed for her sword and shouted, "Look out!" A black shadow separated itself from the bushes and knocked the prince rolling into the forest. The shadow followed before anyone else could react.

"Baoth," shouted Neala, as she charged after the shadow and the prince.

Tíreachán drew his sword and shouted at the others to stay together. They formed a circle near Elise. Amos followed Tír as he dove into the bushes. Suddenly, the circle began to glow again.

"Something is coming out," shouted Meallán. "Get ready." Meallán drew his sword, and Laisrén pulled out his tiny wand. Branna and Turlach reached into their pouches. Branna pulled out a rolling pin, and Turlach produced a metal whisk. Elise blinked as both began to glow with a soft slivery light. They all turned to face the circle. Another shadowy figure came through with a roar.

"Another Phooka!" shouted Laisrén. "Stay together."

The Phooka didn't seem very interested in them but moved to the other side of the circle, keeping an eye on them. It sniffed the air as if it was searching for some particular scent. As it stepped into a patch of moonlight, Elise got her first good look at it and understood why everyone was afraid of these creatures. It was a few inches taller than Prince Rauri, and its muscular body was covered with gray fur. It wore a simple short tunic that was belted with a wide piece of leather. Its features were flat, and the powerful neck and wide shoulders reminded Elise of a catlike gorilla.

"We have to get everyone together and get back through the passageway where our magic is stronger," Turlach said. "Laisrén, see if you can warn the others. Stay high so the Phookas can't get you."

"Obviously," Laisrén muttered as he flew away. The Phooka glanced at him but kept moving around toward the bushes where the others had disappeared.

There was a rustling in the bushes, and Prince Rauri appeared. He stopped short at the sight of the other Phooka.

"Fachtna," he growled. "I was wondering where you would be."

Just then, there was another rustling in the bushes, and Tír came through half carrying Neala who was bleeding from a cut on her side.

"We need to get through," she said as Tír stopped behind the prince. She looked across the circle. "Everyone, go through. Fachtna should follow us. When she does, Elise, you move the stone and close the passageway."

Elise tried to interrupt, but Rauri shook his head. "We can't leave her in your world. Amos is keeping Baoth away but will not be able to for long. Quickly, everyone, through the passageway."

Turlach reached for Fergal as Meallán and Branna stepped into the circle and disappeared into its soft glow. Elise heard a crashing in the bushes and knew Amos was coming back. That meant Baoth was also coming. Suddenly, Turlach cried out and staggered into Elise. She tripped and fell into the circle, holding on to Turlach. She shouted as the Faerie Ring began to glow. This was not the plan.

Elise sat up and stared around her. She was in a cave. A faintly-glowing green circle shone on the wall beside her. Branna rushed over. "Elise, what are you doing here? What happened?"

Before she could answer, the circle glowed bright green, and the prince and Neala came diving through the cave wall. "Everyone back," shouted the prince. "Get out of the cave." They moved away from the glowing wall toward the brightly-lit entrance.

Laisrén zipped through the wall, took one look around, and zipped back through.

"Dratted Fairy," grumbled Neala. "What is he doing?"

Amos came through next, and Elise gasped. He had a cut on his leg and another on his ear. Fergal's jacket was in his mouth, and he was dragging the unconscious Gnome. Laisrén was hanging onto his collar. "You all left Fergal behind," Laisrén complained. "I had to get Amos to help me get him through." He glanced back at the circle. "Tír should be here by now. He was holding off both Phookas but couldn't have lasted much longer."

Finally, Tír came diving through. "Run!" he shouted. "They won't be far behind."

The troupe raced out of the cave. Prince Rauri helped Neala, and Elise followed them, carrying Turlach. Laisrén and Amos, who was still dragging Fergal, came out last. At the edge of the forest, Neala stopped.

"Make a line here," she ordered. "Watch the cave entrance."

They looked back just in time to see one of the Phookas stick its head out of the cave. Neala fired an arrow. There was a cry, and the head disappeared.

"Nicked it," she said pleasantly.

Elise sighed. This was not how she expected to spend the rest of her night. "What happened?" she asked as Amos laid Fergal gently on the ground.

"Baoth must have gotten around Amos and knocked Turlach down. After that, he disappeared again and came out behind us," explained Rauri. "We would have been cut down except for Tíreachán. He ran straight at Baoth. It caught all of us off guard. Fachtna knocked Tír down, but he had distracted both of them long enough for me to get Neala through. I am not sure what happened after that." He turned to Tír.

"Amos jumped across and knocked both of them down," Laisrén interrupted. "Since you all had either fallen or carried other people through, I reminded Amos to get Fergal through and then Tír must have jumped through before he got eaten." He looked at Tíreachán with respect but didn't say anything more.

"He saved us," Neala grumbled. "He seems to be making a habit of that." She didn't seem too happy to have been saved by a Gruagacha. "But we still have a problem." She looked at Elise. "We have to get her back home."

"We cannot defeat them while they are in the cave," said the prince. "There are not enough of us to charge them while they are so protected, and we do not know who else is around. There could be more of them. We will have to go for help."

"We can't leave them, though," said Neala. "We have to block the entrance."

"How will I get back?" demanded Elise. "I have to go back home!"

"There is no help for it," answered Rauri. "Neala is right. We cannot have them following us around. Do not worry," he reassured Elise. "We will get to the castle as quickly as we can, and then we will bring an army of Gnomes to get you back home."

Rauri, Tíreachán, and Meallán set out around the edge of the forest. Neala, Branna, Laisrén, and Elise watched from the tree line.

"Keep down," whispered Laisrén. He pulled out his wand and sent blue magic sizzling into the cave. Nothing looked out.

Suddenly, a few stones trickled down from above the cave entrance. With a loud groan, the front of the cave collapsed, trapping the Phookas inside. Elise sat down and blinked back the tears that rushed into her eyes. She was trapped in the Faerie Realm.

The others came back and looked at their handiwork.

"Hopefully it's not too thick," said Meallán. "We are going to have to undo all this in a few days to get you home." He smiled at Elise.

Elise tried to smile in return, but it quickly faded as she looked closely at the Leprechaun. He was much taller than he had been before. In fact, everyone seemed a lot bigger. "Are you bigger here, or am I smaller?" she asked Meallán, standing up and looking at the rest of the troupe. She was still taller than the prince but guessed she was about half as tall as she was at home. "And why is it day here? It was night at home."

"Time is different here," Meallán answered absently, standing next to Elise and comparing their sizes. "I don't know who has changed size," he finally said. "I feel the same size. You must be smaller." He looked at Amos. "He is smaller, too. Interesting."

By this time, Branna had finished bandaging up Neala. "You will be fine," she said to Neala, "but Fergal is in bad shape." She put her hand on his head. "His side is bleeding again, and I don't know if we got him here quickly enough."

"We have to keep moving," said Prince Rauri. "I do not know why there is no guard at this gate, but something tells me there is trouble here. We cannot expect help to come."

"I can carry him," offered Elise. "I can put him on my back, that way I can carry him easier."

The others agreed and helped get Fergal on Elise's back. She walked carefully to try to keep from jostling him too much. The prince set out through the forest, clearly heading for a specific destination. The others followed without question. Tír carried her backpack, which had somehow gotten smaller as well.

After only a few minutes, they came to a strong-looking stone house in the middle of the woods.

"This is a way station," Branna explained. "They are spread throughout the kingdom, usually near gates to the other realms."

Prince Rauri called out, but the door remained shut. He looked at Laisrén, who grumbled but flew up to an open window on the second floor. Soon, the door opened, but Laisrén looked concerned.

"There's no one here," he said.

"There should always be someone here," said Neala. "It's their job to be here."

"Something must be very wrong for a way station to be abandoned," said Meallán.

Prince Rauri looked grim. "Very wrong indeed," he agreed. "But this is the safest place to stay the night. Let us get settled and decide what to do after we have eaten."

As they opened their packs, Laisrén flew to the window and looked out. "Prince Rauri," he said suddenly, "there is a Fairy camp nearby. Maybe I can get some information."

The prince nodded. "Be careful," he cautioned. "We do not know how much things have changed since we have been absent. If Baoth and Fachtna are both free, then it is likely that Murtagh will also be somewhere about. We do not know who we can trust." Everyone's gaze flickered toward Tíreachán, but no one spoke. Elise noticed but stayed quiet as well. She would ask Branna later.

Laisrén flew out the window, and the rest of the company finished setting up camp. Branna pulled some medicine out of her bag and gave it to Fergal. She shook her head.

"If he doesn't wake up by morning we will have a real problem."

They ate a simple meal, and as they were cleaning up, Laisrén came back. "It's bad," he said abruptly. "Murtagh is back, and he has stolen Doran's bracers."

If Laisrén was hoping for a reaction, the troupe did not disappoint. Everyone gasped. Prince Rauri jumped up demanding more information. Branna dropped the dish she was holding. Only Neala and Tír were still. Tír looked at the ground, and Neala's frozen gaze stabbed briefly in his direction before turning to Laisrén.

Elise's stomach sank at everyone's reactions. "What are bracers?" she asked. "And who is Doran?"

"Bracers are leather arm guards that archers wear," replied Rauri. "These specific bracers are magic. According to legend, the Elven sorcerer Doran enchanted them to focus all of his magic into a concentrated force. No one is exactly sure why he used bracers, but it was probably because they were on a battlefield at the time, and they were right there. Using them, he was able to focus his power into a terrible weapon. The army won the war, but Doran disappeared soon after. The bracers have been locked in the castle armory for centuries."

"Well, they aren't there anymore," continued Laisrén. "Murtagh has them, and he has managed to use them to steal Elf magic."

"That's impossible!" said Neala. "Murtagh is just saying that to scare people."

"That's what everyone thought until he released the wraiths that he created," said Laisrén. "The Fairies told me he puts one bracer on the Elf and one on him and sucks the magic out of them." He paused, and his face became even more serious. "And no one has started coming back."

"What is a wraith, and why do we want them to come back?" asked Elise again. There was very little in this realm that made sense. She felt a prick of tears behind her eyes but blinked them away. At least she was still with everyone. They would get back to the castle, and she would get home soon.

"We are all magical creatures, but our magic comes from different sources," explained Prince Rauri. "Elves draw power from ourselves when we do magic. Gnomes are made of magic, and it is part of their essence. Fairies use wands to channel the magic around them. Brownies make enchanted objects that are not connected to them. Leprechauns use the magic of nature. The Gruagacha cannot safely use magic. For those of us who draw magic from ourselves, we have to be careful to not do too much. If we use too much of our own energy, we become wraiths—like ghosts but a little more substantial."

"Elves become wraiths," said Neala bitterly. "Gruagacha become ghosts if they try even the simplest magic. Stealing a Gnome's magic turns it to stone. Unlike other creatures, we *are* magic."

"How do you come back?" asked Elise again.

"We can only return to our proper forms if there is a tiny sliver of magic left in us," explained Rauri. "We simply have to wait until it grows. Wraiths generally find the strongest magical spots and live there until they become substantial again."

"What if there is not any magic left?" asked Elise.

"Then there is no coming back, and we stay a wraith forever." He thought for a moment. "I am not sure that has ever happened more than a few times in all our history. No matter what they are doing, Elves always hold on to a bit of their magical force, just to make sure they survive. If Murtagh is stealing magic, I do not think he is worried about that."

"But where has he come back from?" asked Elise. "Is he still trying to overthrow the king?"

"Yes," said Laisrén. "Like last time, he claims to be working for the other people of the realm and has promised each group what it most wants. He promised the Pixies and Phookas their own lands over which they could rule as they wanted. He promised the Brownies that they wouldn't have to work for others anymore."

"As if we couldn't just stop if we wanted," snorted Branna.

Prince Rauri took up the story, speaking in a soft voice as if he had heard the news himself. "And for the Gruagacha, he promised to teach them the ancient language, so they could use the magic of the Elves." Rauri paused and looked grim. "Many Gruagacha believed him and joined the Pixies and Phookas to fight against the rest of the realm. They lost. Many of his people were killed in the battle, and the rest were banished with Murtagh into Maon, a dim and silent realm with only one opening into the Faerie Realm."

"How did he get back, then?" asked Meallán. "Did he get through the guard?"

"Not according to him," answered Laisrén. "He claims there is a secret passageway into another realm, and he worked his way back through the uncharted realms. The guards say he must be right because they would never have let him through without a fight."

"What do the Fairies know of his plan?" asked Prince Rauri.

"He has already told King Brian that he has to give up the throne," answered Laisrén. "He said this line of Elves have been ruling the kingdom for too long and things need to change." He looked apologetically at Prince Rauri. "He doesn't seem to have as much support as last time, but the Fairies think that it is only because of the resounding defeat from last time, not because people don't agree with him."

"Let's worry about that in the morning," said Neala. "We need to rest if we are going to do any good tomorrow."

* * * * *

Fergal woke up the next morning, but it was clear he wasn't going to be able to keep up. Turlach also had a large bruise on his leg. He shook his head.

"I will only slow you down," he said. "I will stay here with Fergal, and we will keep watch on the passageway."

"I'll stay also," Branna said. "There should be one healthy person here to take care of you two."

The others said goodbye and shouldered their packs. They continued the discussion from the night before. "If Murtagh is back, then there will be some Gruagacha who want to follow him," Tír said, "but not as many as people think. We do want change, but we don't want things to change through violence."

"What we need is more current information," said Neala. "The Fairies may not have the most recent news. We need to get to Keletvar and the castle and find out what is happening."

"We will have to try to slip in unnoticed," said Rauri. "Murtagh doesn't know we are back, and that gives us the advantage of surprise." He thought for a moment. "If we had some more information, we could take him by surprise and end this before anyone knew we were back."

Neala nodded and actually smiled. "I would love to surprise him at his lair," she said in a cold voice. "Think of how pleased he would be to see us."

Tír looked at Elise and grinned. "I think Neala might be a little too excited about that idea," he whispered just loud enough for Neala to hear. She glared at him but cracked a small smile as she whirled back around.

Except for a quick break for lunch, they walked steadily until dusk. As the others set up camp, Elise sat down with a sigh of relief. She was not used to this much hiking. Aunt Mim and Grams must be worried about her by now. If Kevan found the stone but didn't figure out what had happened, he might take the stone, and she could be stuck here forever. She sniffed a little. Tíreachán came and sat beside her, handing her some food. Meallán watched with a strange expression on his face.

"Don't worry," Tír said kindly. "Time works differently here. You could be here for days, and it would only seem like hours had passed in your world."

"Or the other way around," said Laisrén. "It could be days here and weeks out there. There is no way to know for sure."

"Weeks!" cried Elise. "I can't be gone for weeks! I can't even be gone for a day without Aunt Mim getting upset."

"Let's get some sleep, then," said Neala. "The faster we get to the castle, the faster we can find out what is happening and get you back home."

The next morning, they repacked their bags and started walking again. Late that afternoon, they entered a long, narrow valley that Neala said would lead them within sight of Keletvar. Suddenly, a Phooka came charging out of the trees on the left, followed by a small group of Gruagacha. Neala gave a shout and charged the Phooka.

"Get back," shouted Rauri as he rushed toward the attacking Gruagacha.

Meallán shoved everyone back as another roar came from the forest on the other side of the valley. A second Phooka appeared from the trees, followed by another band of Gruagacha soldiers. Elise grabbed Amos's collar and pulled him away. "We have to hide," she shouted.

Laisrén's sword flashed blue as he shot some magic at the charging Gruagacha. "Head for those thick trees," he said. "We can lose them in there." They raced to the trees followed by the Gruagacha.

Tír pulled his sword and charged the advancing Gruagacha. Elise and Amos ran through the

trees following Meallán. Once they reached the safety of the stand of trees, Elise turned to wait for Tír. She saw Prince Rauri and Neala fighting the two Phookas on the opposite slope. More Gruagacha appeared, and Meallán pulled her further up the hill. Tír retreated and caught up with them.

"We can't let them separate us too much from the others," he gasped. "We have to try to circle around and meet up with them." An arrow thunked into a tree just above his head, and they all ducked.

"I'm kind of like a giant here," said Elise. "I can't sneak very well. How are we going to get around?"

"We run," said Meallán. "If we can get on the other ridge, the prince and Neala can retreat up the hill, and we will be heading toward the castle. We are on the wrong side of the valley."

They gathered their things and started moving. The Gruagacha must have had the same idea, however, and they were pushed further and further away from the prince and Neala. Laisrén flew ahead to find a safe path. They managed to keep out of sight for a few minutes, but soon, a group Gruagacha saw them and charged.

As Tír shouted, "Run!" they gave up on their plan and ran back over the hill. The friends ran blindly until Elise had to stop. Laisrén flew back to see if they were still being followed.

"I don't see anyone coming this way," he said, "but we can't go back the way we came. We will have to go the other way around and see if we can catch the prince and Neala on the other side of the hills. If we get separated too far, though, we may never find them."

"They will head for the castle," said Tír.

"It will take most of the day tomorrow to get to Keletvar," said Meallán. "Especially going the long way around and staying out of the way of the Phookas."

Tíreachán spoke up hesitantly, "I may have a place we can go." He looked around. "I know you all don't trust the Gruagacha, but we can go to my mother's farm. We can stop there before we get to the castle and find out what is going on. If there are armies of Phookas and Gruagacha in the forest, the castle may be in trouble."

"It's better than going in blindly," Meallán agreed. He hesitated. "You may also have trouble getting into the castle without the prince," he said. "It looks like the Gruagacha have joined Murtagh again."

* * * * *

Back in the valley, Prince Rauri and Neala found themselves being slowly pushed toward the hill behind them. They had watched the others run up the hill across the valley and disappear into the trees. Occasionally, a spark of blue magic found its way through the leaves, but soon, they lost all sign of their friends' flight through the woods. The Phookas teamed up and began attacking from either side, forcing the warriors to constantly shift position.

"This isn't going well," Neala shouted as an arrow clanged off her sword. "When more Gruagacha come back, we may have to consider a relocation up the hill a ways."

"Retreat?" asked Rauri with a laugh. "I am surprised that you know how."

"We are just choosing better ground," Neala said as a Phooka rushed her again. "There is a pile of rocks about half way up the hill. If we can make it there, we can fight from some cover." They waited until both Phookas were downhill from their position, giving them a chance to run for the rocks.

"Now!" she called. They raced up the hill and dove behind the rocks. The Phookas growled with frustration but settled in to wait. They had the advantage. When the Gruagacha returned, they would overwhelm the two warriors.

The prince and Neala waited impatiently for the Phookas to move. They had just decided to make a run over the last bit of hill when there was a commotion in the woods on the other side of the valley. The Gruagacha came running back from the woods pursued by an army of Elf and Gnome warriors. The Phookas took one look at the charging army and ran. Neala and Prince Rauri came out of the rocks and waited until one of the Gnome soldiers came up to them. He gasped and bowed.

"Your Highness," he stammered. "We didn't know you were back." He turned to Neala. "Commander Neala, I—" His voice faltered.

"Thank you," said Neala with a small smile. "Tell your captain we would like a word with him."

The soldier saluted and bolted. Prince Rauri smiled. "It seems you are the more terrifying one of us. Poor Gnomeling. He nearly fainted."

Neala smiled. "It's good to know my reputation hasn't suffered from my extended absence."

The officer strode over and bowed to both of them. "Welcome back, Your Highness, commander. You are most definitely a welcome sight."

"Did you see any other travelers on your way?" asked the prince. "You should have passed the rest of our troupe who were running from the Gruagacha army."

"I'm sorry, Your Highness, we saw no one," the man said with a shake of his head. "Perhaps they found a place to hide. Should I send a patrol out to look for them?"

The prince hesitated and looked at Neala. "If you can leave some Gnomes behind to look for them, we would appreciate it. I think we should go to the castle as soon as possible."

The captain nodded and signaled to two of his men. "Take both your squads and search the area to the east," he ordered them. "Who are they looking for?" he asked Neala.

"A Leprechaun, a Fairy, a Gruagacha, a giant human child, and a giant dog," she said briskly.

The men blinked but saluted. "Yes, captain," they said and walked away.

The captain laughed. "That group shouldn't be too hard to track. It will take them a while to find the trail, though. There can't be much left where we came through."

"They should be heading to the castle as well," said Neala. "We will likely find them there soon."

"If you have any healers," Prince Rauri added, "we left some wounded comrades at the way station near the cave. It had been abandoned, and two Phookas are trapped in the passage cave." He stopped and considered. "Though, perhaps it is better to leave them there for the time being. Commander Fergal is wounded and would benefit from any help you can give him."

The captain nodded. "I will send whatever help we can, along with some soldiers to man the way station and keep an eye on the cave." He saluted and walked away to give the orders.

Neala looked at the prince with a frown. "Do we go to the castle or look for the others?" she asked again.

Prince Rauri looked across the valley, his brow wrinkled in thought. "The castle," he said finally. "The others will try to get there as well. If they were pushed far enough into the hills, they will find it easier to go around the other way. We may well find them waiting for us when we get there."

Neala nodded. "If they make it," she said darkly.

* * * * *

Prince Rauri and Neala joined the Gnome army as they returned to the castle. The patrols hadn't found any sign of the rest of the troupe but, as Neala pointed out to the prince, "Meallán and Laisrén will know what to do."

"I am worried about Tír being caught up in all of this," Prince Rauri said, looking toward the woods where their friends had disappeared. "I do not like the size of the Gruagacha army Murtagh has managed to assemble again." He looked around at the Gnomes traveling with them. "There are no Gruagacha with this army. There should be some, at least. There are many loyal Gruagacha," he said, almost to himself.

Neala shrugged. "If they stay off the main roads, they will be fine. We will find them soon."

They traveled through the night. When they arrived at the castle the next morning, they were met with shouting and commotion.

"This doesn't sound good," said the captain. "Be ready as you go in!" he commanded. The Gnomes loosened their swords and trotted into the open castle gate.

"Prince Rauri!" a voice called. The captain of the guard ran over to meet them. "You're back. You must come to the king at once!" he said as he bowed to the prince.

"What happened?" Rauri asked.

"I'll let the king tell you," he said, bowing to Neala as well.

They marched into the castle and into the throne room. King Brian was standing in the middle of a group of Elves and Gnomes who were all shouting at each other.

"Silence!" the king ordered. He looked up and closed his eyes with relief. "Prince Rauri, at last. Your arrival could not be at a more desperate hour."

"Your Majesty," Rauri said, as he and Neala bowed. "What has happened?"

"Murtagh!" shouted the king, suddenly angry again. "Murtagh has kidnapped Princess Líoch, and Queen Keeva was taken while trying to rescue her."

"How did this happen?" Rauri asked. "How did he get inside the castle?"

"He did not get in," said King Brian grimly. "A group of Gruagacha posing as servants managed to get into the princess's room. They put that abominable bracer on her, and she immediately collapsed. They were sighted as they were trying to get to the court-yard to escape using Pixie dust. Just as they made it clear, Queen Keeva grabbed one of them and disappeared in the dust with them."

"That had to be a nasty surprise when they arrived," said Neala with a smirk. Queen Keeva's magical powers were legendary in the Faerie Realm.

King Brian gave a short laugh. "I imagine so, but we have no way of knowing what happened. Unless they could find some Pixie dust, they might not be able to return. Until we hear something, we have to assume they have both been captured. If he puts that bracer on Keeva, he will have a lot of power at his command."

"We should organize a troupe to go after them," said the prince. "Do you have any idea where they might have gone?"

"Somewhere in the northern mountains is all we know so far," said the captain. "The wraiths that have made it back have been quite vague about where they came from."

"Then we will search all of the mountains until we find them," said the prince.

"We have sent out patrols to monitor the Gruagacha and watch for any signs that they are in league with Murtagh," said the king. "I thought they had learned from last time that they have no hope of defeating us."

"I am not sure they care about defeating us," said the prince thoughtfully. "I think they are just trying to get our attention."

"Well, they have it now!" shouted the king. "Search the area around the city. He may not have taken them very far." He pointed at one of the soldiers standing near the door. "Go inform the army."

The soldier saluted and hurried out the door.

Murtagh waited in a farmhouse just outside Keletvar. He looked around, remembering his childhood on a farm much like this one. The Elves thought the Gruagacha were weak and easily oppressed, but he would show them. This time, he would succeed. The Gruagacha had once again let their desire for equality lead them into rebelling against the king. King Brian would be furious and would strike out against all the Gruagacha, regardless of whether or not they had been involved. This would bring more Gruagacha to his side and give him the army he needed to defeat the Elves and their allies. His Gruagacha spies should be back any minute with the princess. Once he showed he was serious in his threats, King Brian would have to listen.

There was a glimmer of Pixie dust, and then, the group appeared. Princess Líoch cried out as the Gruagacha dropped her on the ground. "Welcome, Princess—" Murtagh's oily greeting was cut short. His smile froze and then crumbled as Queen Keeva appeared behind the Gruagacha.

She spoke one word, and they collapsed.

Murtagh responded with a shout, and the princess cried out in surprise and pain. Keeva froze, looking at the bracer on her daughter's arm. "How did you get here?" Murtagh snarled. This was a big problem.

"Did you think you could take my daughter so easily?" the queen demanded. "Let her go."

Murtagh raised his arm which was encased in the matching bracer. "I don't think you want to get into a magical battle right now,

Your Majesty. Your daughter won't last long in a battle of that magnitude." He smiled at the queen's hesitation.

"But neither can I allow you to destroy the Faerie Realm because of your greed," she said. She raised her hands and, with a sorrowful look at her daughter, said, "Megszédít."

Murtagh jumped behind his guards as a bolt of power came charging at him. He managed to get a defensive shield up but not in time to save the guards. They tumbled against the walls leaving Murtagh exposed. Murtagh shouted in response as he ducked to the side.

Queen Keeva was already moving and speaking words with each step, power flaring from her hands. The princess cried out once more and then lay still. Suddenly, the queen stopped mid-word and collapsed. A Phookah holding a large club appeared in the doorway behind her, sneering.

"Your timing is impeccable," Murtagh said with a small shiver. "That was about to get interesting." He motioned to the Gruagacha, who had taken cover during the magical battle. "This is better than I had planned. With her power, I think a small change of plan is in order." He removed the bracer from the princess and put it on the queen. "Bring the letter. I must add a suitable postscript." He chuckled as he wrote his message with a flourish.

"You have one minute," he said, handing the letter to a hovering Pixie. "If you are too slow, you will be trapped in there with everyone else." He grinned at the Pixie. "I'm sure they would try very hard to catch you, and you wouldn't be able to bargain your way out with mere gifts of dust."

The Pixie vanished, and Murtagh tested the connection with the queen. He felt an immediate swell of power. Queen Keeva was one of the most powerful Elves in the realm. With her power, he would be nearly invincible. Instead of threatening, he would simply force the king to obey his commands, and then, after the Pixies transported them back to the mountain, he would gather his army for the final battle. With both the princess and the queen taken, King Brian would undoubtedly take his anger out on the Gruagacha. This would force them to choose his side. Soon, his army would be bigger than ever, and with the queen's magic, nothing could stop him.

* * * * *

Pacing irritably in the throne room, King Brian continued to shout out orders. Suddenly, a Pixie appeared in the middle of the group, fluttering above their heads and giggling ominously. It dropped a letter to the king and disappeared.

King Brian read the letter aloud.

"King Brian, I assume, by now, you are planning to scour the kingdom in search of your daughter. You won't."

The king stopped and bellowed with rage, "Who does he think he is giving me orders like this?"

Shaking with wrath, he continued.

> Any attempt to rescue her will result in her being turned into a wraith—immediately and permanently. You shall hear from me shortly at which time you will abdicate your throne, and a new king will be chosen by the popular demand of my growing army. Your tyranny is at an end, and we will have a new rule with equal rights for all.
>
> Sincerely, Murtagh

> P.S. With the surprise addition of your lovely wife, I have taken the liberty of using her power to create a barrier around the castle. Now, you simply can't leave. The amount of power it takes to sustain this barrier should be sufficient to keep the queen under control. A bit draining for her, but she is holding on.

The king went pale. "Someone check the gate. See if this is true."

One of the guards ran for the door just as it burst open. The soldier he had sent out earlier had come back.

"Your Majesty," the man called. "There is some kind of spell around the gate. We can speak through the barrier, but no one can get in or out."

King Brian nodded. He turned to the captain of his personal guard. "Try Pixie dust or any other way you can think of to find a way out." The man nodded and hurried away. The king turned to Rauri and Neala. "Come with me. We must see if we can figure out where Murtagh is hiding. As soon as we find a way out, we will be ready to move."

"Wait, Your Majesty," Neala said with a frown. "Who is in this growing army he is talking about? If he gets a large-enough force, he could be difficult to stop."

The king looked at the letter again. "The same people as last time," he muttered. "Murtagh will gather the Pixies and Phookas and the Gruagacha, along with any other malcontent he can find." He crumpled the letter and looked at the marshal, the leader of the army. "Assemble any soldiers we have outside the barrier. No Gruagacha are to assemble in groups. They are to stay strictly in their homes or on their farms. Anyone who does not cooperate will be confined in the mines. They will not be able to join him this time."

Prince Rauri glanced at Neala and motioned for her to slip away. He made his way through the crowd that was milling around the king. "We have to try to warn Tír," he said. "He will be sneaking around trying to find out what has been happening and will look suspicious."

Neala shrugged. "There isn't much we can do. We are stuck in here, and it's not like we can send him a message. They are on their own." She grimaced. "We have to trust that they won't do something stupid and get caught."

"But this will have the exact effect that Murtagh wants," argued Rauri. "Think about it, Neala. Even Tír would fight if the soldiers enforce these rules. This will make the Gruagacha hate us more than ever."

"I don't see what we can do," Neala countered. "King Brian has made up his mind. He has to remove any chance of threat."

"The Gruagacha are not a threat unless we force them to be," Rauri said, throwing his hands in the air. "They just want to be treated like everyone else. Is that so hard for everyone to see?"

Neala looked at him in astonishment. "They kidnapped the princess—your fiancée," she said. "How can you be on their side?"

"Some of them did that," said the prince. "You cannot arrest a whole race of Faerie because some of them broke the law."

King Brian bellowed for silence, and the prince and Neala turned to listen again. "Call in all your outer patrols," he said to his generals. "Those not keeping an eye on the Gruagacha will be preparing for Murtagh's return. He has to come here in order to take the throne, and then we will have the best chance of ending this once and for all."

He turned and strode from the room, leaving his generals to carry out his orders. Prince Rauri followed him hoping to get him to reconsider. Neala shrugged. King Brian rarely changed his mind, and this didn't seem to be a day where that would happen. She went out to look around and try her own ways of getting out of the castle.

Elise was tired after their escape from the Gruagacha army, but Tír only allowed them a short rest before he got them up.

"We have to get to the castle. If something happened to the prince and Neala, then we have to figure out how to get Elise home."

"If anything happened to them," Laisrén grumbled, "we may have bigger trouble than getting her home. We may have to worry about having a power-stealing lunatic as our king."

"Enough time to worry about that when we find out what happened," said Meallán. "Tír's right. Let's worry about getting to the castle first." Tír looked a bit surprised at this support from the Leprechaun but nodded.

"We'll walk for a few more hours before we stop for the night," he said. "I wish we knew where the army was. Either army. I don't want to run into a Phooka in the dark."

"Isn't there any kind magic we can use?" asked Elise. "I thought once we got here, you could use magic."

Meallán shrugged. "Leprechauns don't have any kind of magic that can transport us. Our magic is more for hiding or sneaking around stealing sparkly things." He grinned as Elise glared at him. "Don't worry," he said. "I gave everything back. I don't steal from friends."

"Unless we were in a very strong magical spot, I could only take a group this big a short distance," said Laisrén. "And it isn't the most secretive way to travel. The flash that spell would make would let everyone know exactly where we were."

Tír shrugged. "Then we walk," he said. "Just because this is the Faerie Realm, it doesn't mean that magic can solve every problem."

They set off, keeping to the forest and smaller roads until they found a safe place to sleep. Under the drooping branches of a pine tree, they passed an uneasy night listening for any sound of the Gruagacha army.

Elise shivered as Laisrén cheerfully pointed out, "We probably wouldn't hear a Phooka until it was attacking anyway, so we needn't bother keeping watch for them."

* * * * *

Elise groaned as she rolled over the next morning. Amos licked her face encouragingly. "I know," Elise grumbled. "You are having a great time. But I'm not used to sleeping on the ground."

"We should be able to sleep comfortably tonight," Tír encouraged her. "All we have to do is walk there!"

It was a long walk to Tíreachán's farm. Laisrén took the opportunity to tell Elise a number of improbable stories where the heroes were victorious at the last minute "by magic." It seemed that every problem apart from traveling could be solved by magic here.

Finally, they had to march in silence. The farms were closer together, and there was a greater risk of being seen. After a number of close calls, Tír decided that they should stay hidden for the rest of the day and make their way to the farm after dark. They found a secluded place and made camp.

As the sun set, they gathered their belongings and Tíreachán took the lead as they moved through the forest. Finally, they came to a small farm. The snug little house was set back off the road, and the barn was tucked back at the edge of the forest. The fields across the road from the house waved with some kind of grass that Elise didn't recognize in the darkness. They snuck around and waited in the barn while Tír went to find his mother. He slipped back in after a moment.

"She will come soon," he said softly.

A few minutes later, a small door opened, and a woman entered the barn. She was carrying a bucket in each hand and shut the door briskly behind her. She froze as Amos trotted over to check out the buckets.

Tíreachán hurried to make introductions. "Mother, this is the human, Elise, and her dog, Amos, who were trapped in our realm after helping us find our way back." His mother gasped at this introduction and stared at Elise, who was pulling at Amos's collar.

"Stop it, Amos," she scolded. "You are a giant dog here. Stop scaring people."

Amos dropped to the floor with a sigh and turned his sad eyes toward the buckets, hoping for some food. Tír took advantage of the pause to continue his introductions. "This is Meallán and Laisrén. And this is my mother, Teagan," he finished with a rush, waving his hand toward his mother.

"Welcome," Teagan finally said, looking up at Elise. "I don't know how you ended up in our realm, but thank you for helping bring my son home." She gave Amos a careful pat on the head and looked at the others. "Welcome, all of you, to our home. I can't offer you proper hospitality, but I have brought some food, and I will try to do what I can."

Meallán stepped forward. "Thank you for your help," he said. "We know Murtagh is back but nothing else. What news can you tell us?"

"Nothing good," said Teagan, handing the buckets of food to Tír. As he put the food in their packs, Teagan told them about the princess and the Gruagacha who had helped Murtagh. "King Brian blames us for supporting that madman, but all he cares about is that we keep working like nothing happened," she said bitterly. "The army has orders to arrest any Gruagacha found in groups or acting in any suspicious manner, which could mean anything right now."

"How are the Gruagacha taking this news?" asked Laisrén. "They can't be too happy about it. Isn't it pushing them to support Murtagh?"

"Some," admitted Teagan. "More and more Gruagacha are becoming impatient for change. They were afraid to try force after Murtagh's last uprising, but now that he is back, people are starting to change their minds."

"What do you think?" asked Meallán carefully.

"Nothing will be gained even if Murtagh does manage to take the throne," said Teagan. "All that will do is start a war that will never end. Each side will continue to try to reclaim the throne from the other until we have destroyed ourselves. In this matter, peaceful change is the only way to truly have a victory."

"Then we have to stop Murtagh," said Tír. "If we can find him and rescue the queen and the princess, he won't have any leverage against the king, and the queen will be able to defeat him."

"Are you crazy?" shouted Laisrén. "How could we stop Murtagh? We aren't warriors. We are a Fairy, a Leprechaun, and a Gruagacha who is going to be arrested if he starts wandering around asking for directions to Murtagh's lair."

"We are also a human, who happens to be kind of a giant here, and a giant dog," interrupted Elise. She had been listening to the discussion with growing dread. It seemed like she wasn't going to get home any time soon. "I can't wait for a whole war to finish before I go home," she said with a tiny sob. "If we have to find the queen to stop Murtagh, then that's what we should do."

Amos growled and then sighed. It seemed he agreed, though he wasn't very happy about it.

Teagan patted Elise's hand. "Don't worry, dear," she said kindly. "As it happens, I agree with you." She turned and looked at Tír. "And I will come with you. I think I can be of some help."

"Does anyone know where Murtagh is hiding?" asked Tír, looking uncertainly at his mother.

"No one knows for sure where he is right now, but most of the wraiths remember coming from the northwest. The forest there is filled with Pixies, and a few Phookas have even been seen. I believe he is hiding somewhere in the northern mountains. Elves and even Gnomes rarely go there, and there are many places to hide." She shook her head. "Murtagh has always claimed to be doing these things for the good of others, but really, he has never cared for anyone but himself."

"How do you know so much about him?" asked Meallán.

"I know more about him than anyone," admitted Teagan. "Murtagh isn't an Elf like everyone thinks. He is a Gruagacha."

"A Gruagacha?" Laisrén asked. "That's impossible! No Gruagacha could do magic like that."

"It is true," Teagan said. "I don't know why he has never told anyone, but I knew him before he became the magician he is now." She looked apologetically at Tíreachán before continuing. "He is my brother."

"Your brother? He's my uncle?" asked Tír in disbelief. "Why didn't you ever tell me?" He stopped in confusion. "How did he learn the ancient language?" he demanded.

"He went to work for an elderly Elf when he was young," explained Teagan. "He convinced the Elf to teach him a bit and snuck around learning as much as he could. I don't know how he learned so much, but it probably wasn't a nice way." She looked at them seriously. "He could never accept the fact that the Elves wouldn't let us learn. Ever since we were very young, he has made it his goal to steal as much knowledge as he could to use against the Elves."

"Why didn't you ever tell anyone?" demanded Tír. "It proves that the Gruagacha can do magic! The Elves would have to believe us."

"Would they?" asked Teagan. "What proof do I have? Besides, Murtagh is not a great example of what the Gruagacha would do with magic. Would that knowledge spark a revolution? Would people be more willing to fight if they learned a bit of magic? It might destroy everything we have been working for all these years."

Suddenly, Amos growled, and Laisrén flew up to the window. "Someone is coming," he said. "A lot of them."

"Stay here and keep quiet," ordered Teagan. "I will get rid of them as quickly as I can."

A large crowd was gathering in front of the house. One man stepped up and quieted the group. "Teagan!" he called. "It has started. The Elves and Gnome soldiers are taking our friends and neighbors away. We had nothing to do with what happened at the castle, but we are being punished simply because we are Gruagacha! It's time to do something!"

Teagan made her way through the crowd to turn their attention away from the barn. Tír and the others peeked through a crack in the door.

"What have the Elves ever done for us?" the man continued. "They made us who we are! They stopped us from learning magic and made us their servants!" The crowd grumbled in agreement. "Murtagh may be crazy, but at least we will get what we want. I say if he will teach us the ancient language, we should support him." The crowd started shouting in agreement.

Teagan stood up, and the crowd turned to look at her. "You are all fools!" she shouted.

Tíreachán snorted. "That's my mother," he said fondly.

Laisrén laughed. "The one who called the angry mob a bunch of fools? Right. Of course that's your mother."

"But look," said Meallán, "they are listening to her."

The crowd had simmered down and was waiting for her to continue.

"What did Murtagh promise last time? Freedom from Elvish rule? Well, those who followed him got that. There were no Elves where they ended up. And who made it back from that? Don't you think it is a little bit suspicious that of all the people who were banished, so few came back? None of our people made it back." There was a small murmur of agreement. She was a convincing speaker. "Now, I agree that things need to change. The Elves are wrong to keep us poor and uneducated—" The murmur grew louder and cut her off. "However," her strong voice quieted them down, "getting what we want through violence makes us just as bad as them. And what does it teach our children? The only way to solve a problem is to take what you want by force? That will lead to an ugly world. We may not agree with King Brian, and we may not like the Elves, but that doesn't mean we want them all turned to wraiths forever."

The crowd was silent. The first man tried to speak again, but Teagan stopped him. "Enough. These last threats are just too much. Are we going to support someone who would kidnap the queen and princess and turn them into wraiths? Is that how we want to be remembered? I want nothing to do with him. He has never cared about anyone other than himself, and he isn't about to change now."

"Neither is the king!" shouted the first man. "We have sent requests and asked again and again for a better life. What response have we gotten? Nothing! King Brian is so stuck following the traditions of the realm, that he will never consider our requests."

Before the crowd could decide what to do, there was a commotion in the woods. A troupe of Gnomes and Elves appeared from the darkness.

"You are all under arrest for treason against the king," the Elf captain shouted. He looked at the two Gruagacha standing at the front of the crowd and stiffened. "You!" he said, pointing at Teagan. "Seize that Gruagacha! She was one of his followers last time."

Tír cried out as the crowd scattered into the night. The Gnomes caught many of them, including Teagan and the Gruagacha who had been speaking. Tír tried to open the door, but Meallán stopped him. "You will just get arrested, too. Probably all of us will. If Prince Rauri hasn't made it back, it will take a miracle for us to find someone who knows who we are."

"Search the barn!" the captain shouted.

"No!" Teagan cried. "Run!" she shouted. She wrenched one arm free from the soldier's grasp and pointed at the ground in front of the barn. "Szakédek!" she shouted. Soldiers scattered along with the Gruagacha as the ground split open and a widening crack cut them off from the barn. The ground fell away and everyone ran for safety.

Tír gaped in amazement as his mother continued speaking. The crack carried on into the woods. The barn was cut off.

"Silence her!" the captain shouted. "She is working with Murtagh. How else could she know the ancient language?" One of the Gnomes clapped his hand over Teagan's mouth as another found a scarf to silence her. The ground rumbled to a standstill.

"Let's go," whispered Laisrén. "It won't take them long to get around that crack to find out who she was protecting. We need to get as far away from here as possible."

Everyone grabbed their packs and followed Tír out the back door. He led the way through the woods away from the shouting crowd of Gruagacha and the Gnomes who were rounding them up.

They kept moving through the night. Finally, as the sky began to lighten, Elise could not go on any longer, and Laisrén flew ahead to find a place for them to rest. He found a small hollow that had formed under a giant fallen tree. Meallán handed out some of the food Tír's mother had given them as they discussed what to do. Suddenly, Elise choked and looked at her food in horror.

"What's the matter?" asked Tíreachán.

"I forgot!" cried Elise. "My uncle told me that I shouldn't eat food from the Faerie Realm or I would get stuck here forever. We were eating food from home before, so I forgot all about it."

Everyone stared at the food in her hand. "Don't worry," Meallán reassured her, glancing at Tír and Laisrén. "Between the king and the queen, someone will find a solution. Together, they can do pretty much anything."

Elise nodded but couldn't take another bite. All her work to get home might be ruined because she had forgotten Uncle Jake's warning. She looked in her bag for other food from home. She just hoped Meallán was right and they had both the king and the queen helping them at the end of all this.

"We need a plan," said Laisrén, breaking the silence. "What are we going to do?"

"If Prince Rauri is alive, he must be in the castle," said Meallán. "We should try to contact him and let him know we are here. He can tell us what to do."

"I won't be able to move freely around Keletvar after tonight," said Tír. "I think we should try to find Murtagh and rescue the princess and the queen." He stopped as Meallán and Laisrén protested. "Prince Rauri and Neala had the same idea. Murtagh doesn't know we even exist. He is watching the castle and the army. We might be able to sneak in and get them without him even knowing."

"That was Neala and the prince," argued Laisrén. "They might have been able to surprise Murtagh and save his true love and restore peace and order to the realm, but we don't have a chance of doing any of that without dying."

"Isn't the princess his sister?" asked Elise, frowning in confusion. "If he is the prince and she is the princess, they are brother and sister."

"It's not that simple," Meallán explained. "The king had a son, but he disappeared. Since Rauri and the princess were already in love, the king made Rauri the crown prince."

"Not important!" Laisrén shouted. "The important thing is that we get some actual help and let *them* stop Murtagh without us getting killed."

Amos growled, and Elise stroked his head. She didn't want to give up, but she agreed with Laisrén on this one. They weren't warriors or heroes. "Maybe Laisrén should go to the castle," she suggested in a whisper. "We can't do this without help."

"Let's rest for a while and see what we think of," Meallán suggested. "We can't keep running until we know where we are going."

Everyone agreed and lay down, trying to get as comfortable as possible on the bare ground. Elise fell asleep almost immediately, her hand resting on Amos's side. He was the only thing she had left from her world. She had to get back.

When she woke up, the sun was high in the sky. Laisrén and Meallán were at the far side of camp whispering furiously. When they noticed that she was awake, they turned to Tír and Elise. "We have a plan," Meallán began.

"A risky plan," interjected Laisrén.

"But a good risky plan," argued Meallán. This seemed to be the point of contention between them.

"Let's hear it," said Tír. "We have no plan now besides walking to the northern mountains and hoping for a bit of luck or walking into Keletvar, where everyone wants to arrest me, and our only friends are stuck in the castle."

"Your only friends," mumbled Laisrén. "I have lots of friends."

"Since it seems that going back to the castle will not accomplish anything useful, I suggest asking the Adaros for help finding Murtagh," Meallán said grandly.

"They don't help anyone," said Tír skeptically. "They are more likely to throw water on us than do anything helpful."

"Not all of them," argued Meallán. "The Leprechauns are friends with them, and they often help us travel around, even between realms. I have a friend who may agree to help us. They don't want Murtagh in charge any more than the rest of us. We can travel by rainbow as far as they can get us into the forest near the mountains." He paused. "Once we are there, things get a little tricky." He looked at Laisrén.

"We find a Pixie for Elise to capture," said Laisrén with a grin.

Elise sat in stunned silence for a moment and then burst out, "Why me?"

"It will be easiest for you," answered Meallán. "Pixies love teasing humans, and they won't suspect that you know about catching them. Amos can go with you in case anything goes wrong."

"Why would I want to catch a Pixie?" asked Elise.

"If you capture a Pixie, it will give you a gift of Pixie dust as ransom," said Laisrén. "They can magic the dust to do whatever they want it to do. You have to be firm and specific though, or it will try to trick you."

"What you want," explained Meallán, "is to get the Pixie to give you some Pixie dust that will lead you to the princess." He thought for a moment. "Or maybe dust that will take you wherever you tell it to go. That way, we can decide what to do once we've got it."

"How will I catch one?" asked Elise.

"There is no good way to catch one," replied Laisrén. "That's why almost no one ever tries. If they suspect you are trying to catch them, they will attack. They are small, but they are nasty. It's never a good idea to cross a horde of Pixies."

"I have a better idea," said Tíreachán suddenly. "What if Amos catches a Pixie, and Elise rescues it? It will be safer for Amos to have a horde of Pixies angry at him than for Elise."

Amos growled at the Gruagacha, but Laisrén nodded. "Good idea. It's easier to deal with a Pixie you've rescued than one you've captured." He looked at Elise. "The rules for Pixies you've rescued are pretty much the same, but they are much happier rewarding you with Pixie dust than giving it up as a ransom. The rest of us will stay hidden until Elise has the Pixie dust. If the Pixies don't cooperate, we will just have to take the chance of provoking the horde and all try to catch one."

Amos snorted but seemed to go along with the plan. Elise hoped he knew what he was doing. She didn't like the idea of being swarmed by a horde of angry Pixies.

* * * * *

To save time, Laisrén took the risk of a transportation spell. The flash of blue light was blinding, but the mountains were much closer when Elise blinked away the last of the flashing lights.

"We should get moving," Tír said, rubbing his eyes. "With everything that is going on, you can be sure that someone from both sides is going to investigate a flash that big. Everyone is going to be wondering what the Fairies are up to."

"Let them wonder," said Laisrén with a short laugh. "It will do both sides some good to worry about us for once."

His transportation spell had been accurate, and the Adaros' pool wasn't far. Meallán took the lead and explained to Elise where they were going. "The Adaros are sort of fish-men," he began. "Not really like merpeople because they are more fish than human. They live in the water, but they prefer to travel by rainbow."

"Uh, they sound lovely, I guess," said Elise.

"They are horrible, grumpy creatures," interrupted Laisrén from behind.

"They aren't horrible," disagreed Meallán. "They don't like other folks much, though they are friendly with the Leprechauns.

We try to help them out whenever we can. Every once in a while, they fall out of their rainbows and need a hand getting back in. The Adaro I'm hoping to find is called Corc. I helped him out one time when he fell out of a rainbow in the Human Realm."

"Do they travel to the Human Realm often?" asked Elise with surprise. "I've never heard of them."

"They are very small in your realm," said Meallán. "They travel all over. More than most of the Faerie, except maybe Gnomes. They live near a great waterfall that comes down from Mount Caylyn." He pointed to the mountain in front of them, its peak lost in the clouds. "There is always mist from the waterfall so there is always a rainbow. Once the Adaros get into the air, there is usually enough moisture for them to move around. They can't go anywhere that is very dry, though, so I'm not sure how far they can take us into the northern forest."

They heard the waterfall long before they saw it. As they came around the curve of the valley, Elise was surprised to see the waterfall coming straight down from the hidden mountain peak.

"Where does the water come from?" asked Elise. "It doesn't seem like there could be a river that big on top of a mountain that high."

"Magic," smirked Laisrén.

Elise rolled her eyes. She knew this was the Faerie Realm, but she just wished one explanation didn't end with "magic."

As they came nearer to the pool below the waterfall, Elise saw strange creatures that had to be the Adaros. They were clearly fish but with fins that flared out into humanlike arms that connected to their bodies with a thin membrane up to the elbow. Their fishy-human heads joined their bodies with no trace of a neck. Although no one turned, Elise felt the bulging eyes watching as the troupe come up behind them.

The Adaros were lying on the rocks on the shallow edge of the pool, some half out of the water, dozing in the sunshine. The variety of size and color reminded Elise of her visit to the aquarium last year.

One Adaro finally acknowledged their presence by shouting, "Go away! We don't want your kind around here! We don't grant wishes to hoodlums." He jumped into the deep-blue water and swam to the waterfall. To Elise's amazement, he swam straight up the water and out of sight. Many of the other Adaros jumped into the water and swam to the other side of the pool or disappeared under the churning waterfall. The few who were left ignored them so pointedly that Elise suspected they had stayed just so that they could ignore them.

Meallán, with no sign of shock at their rude behavior, walked over to one of the Adaros. The long, green fish-man opened one eye and growled, "What do you want, greenie?"

Meallán smiled and replied, "I was merely wondering if you know Corc. I'm Meallán, and I'm here to visit him."

The Adaro grunted and finally replied, "He's been around. I'm not going to go find him for you, but if you wait, maybe he will swim past soon." He closed his eyes again, and Elise studied him in fascination. His head was blunt and almost squarish. A long, bluish-green fin ran down his back, the coloring blending into his green body and fading to yellow-green on his stomach. His arm-fins were slightly stubby compared to his broad shape, which tapered down to his split tail fin.

"Thank you," Meallán replied and sat on a nearby stone, his feet swinging over the water. He motioned for the others to sit.

"Are we really going to just wait for him to *maybe* swim past?" Tír whispered to Meallán as he sat in the grass near the pool.

The Adaro heard him and snorted. "This is the problem with you big people. You are so used to everything happening so quickly you can't wait two minutes for the common Adaro."

"They have sent a message to him," whispered Meallán with a smile. "They just don't want anyone to know they care."

"We don't care about any of you!" shouted the Adaro. "You just try to knock us out of our rainbows, so you can pretend to do us a favor and get your wish. Well, it won't work! We don't grant wishes to ruffians."

"Since we are waiting," said Meallán casually, motioning for everyone to be quiet, "I wonder if any Adaros have noticed anything strange happening in your travels."

The green Adaro glared at him. "You mean besides that crazy Elf magician setting wraiths whirling around everywhere, blocking our sunlight? It's a wonder we can get anywhere to notice anything these days." He glared at Tír. "You Gruagacha are just causing trouble for all of us by following him again."

Tír jumped up and grabbed his sword. Meallán grabbed his wrist as the Adaro started to slide into the pool. "We do not all support Murtagh," replied Tír with a slight edge to his voice. "All we want is to be treated equally. Most of us don't like Murtagh any more than you do."

The Adaro, pretending to be unconcerned about the angry Gruagacha looming over him, continued, "It's not safe to leave the pool anymore. The wraiths are wreaking havoc on our rainbows. Every time they fly past, they cause a disruption. We've had to promise wishes to every third person that walks by." He glared at the group. "I suppose you want us to do something to help."

Just then, another head popped up from the pool. This Adaro was bright red with black eyes. He glared at Meallán. "I already gave you your chance to have a wish. It's not my fault you've ignored the offer all this time." He glanced at the group and then looked even more irritable. "This looks like some kind of quest. I suppose you think you can just show up here any time you want to get somewhere without walking."

"Hello, Corc," replied Meallán blandly. "This is Tíreachán and Laisrén, along with the human, Elise, and her dog, Amos." Corc glared at them all and firmly closed his mouth, staunchly refusing to give any greeting. "We were hoping you could do us the service of taking us to the northern forest. We have reason to believe that Murtagh is hiding somewhere near there."

"I knew it!" said the green Adaro grimly. "Straight into danger. The rainbows won't go there," he added with glee. "You can't make it."

"Nevertheless, we must try," said Tír firmly. "Murtagh has kidnapped the queen and the princess. We must try to get them back."

"Well," Corc said gruffly, "if it will make you go away, I suppose I'll have to get you there. We can't have you hanging around waving your sword every time you get excited."

The green Adaro splashed his tail in irritation. "With this large of a group and the giant human, you'll need at least three Adaros. Now, we'll have to find someone else to come with us."

"You're coming?" exclaimed Elise in surprise. "And I'm not a giant!"

"Of course I'm coming!" shouted the green Adaro. "You've interrupted my nap. The fastest way to get back to sleep is to get you out of here. If you aren't happy, you'll just sit around complaining the whole time. And if you aren't a giant, why are you so much taller than everyone else?"

Elise blinked at the pace of the Adaro's conversation, but before she could figure out which part of his speech to reply to, a black, whiskery face popped out of the pool.

"Will you stop all this chatter? I suppose I'll have to come along just to get some peace and quiet around here. Some people have no respect for the peace and quiet of others." Elise stared at the newest

Adaro. He had long slimy strands dangling from his face and, with a sudden shock, Elise realized that this was a catfish. The black Adaro caught her look and made a sour face. Elise tried not to stare but studied the other Adaros to see if she could recognize any other fish as well.

Meallán grinned and winked at Tír. "I suppose this will have to do," he agreed. "We'll probably get soaked and end up somewhere completely different from where we want to go, but poor help is better than none."

"Wait," interrupted Tír, "if they can travel between realms, can't they get Elise home?"

Elise felt a surge of relief, immediately followed by disappointment. "But I want to help," she protested. "I can at least help you catch the Pixie, and then I can go home."

"Won't work," said the Adaro. "We are too small in the Human Realm, and you are too big. I mean, we can get you to the Human Realm, but chances are, you will break the rainbow." He smirked. "If you're desperate, an ocean Adaro might be able to get you there, but it might eat you instead. They aren't as pleasant as we freshwater Adaros. Too salty."

"No, thanks," Elise said. She didn't want to be eaten or take the chance of falling out of a rainbow.

The Adaro grunted, and one more head popped up, this one much lighter and more pointed than the others. As he came further out of the water, Elise saw a red stripe down his side. He must be a rainbow trout, she decided. His arm-fins were even shorter than the green Adaro's, and Elise giggled as he waved them in annoyance.

"Just get going!" he shouted. "I suppose you think with four of us, you can get there faster. I just want to keep the rest of your kinds out of our pool. Let's get moving."

The four Adaros lined up at the edge of the pool glaring at the group and muttering to each other. The group looked at Meallán for help. "Hold on to anything you don't want to lose," he instructed. "Once we get moving, we will go pretty fast, but they have everything under control."

"Of course we do," one of the Adaros interrupted. "You'd think we'd never carried a load of ruffians down our rainbows. That Fairy is a problem, though. There is enough magic residue floating around him to throw things off." He glared at Laisrén, who grabbed his tiny wand and glared back.

Tír and Meallán strapped their packs on firmly and held on to their weapons. Elise tightened her backpack straps and reached for Amos's collar. She could manage without anything else as long as she had Amos. The Adaros slapped their tails on the water to create a spray of drops that twinkled in the sun. Suddenly, Elise felt like she was being sucked into a waterslide. The world flickered by, shimmering through the bubble of water surrounding them. The four Adaros, now one at each corner of the group, continued to flick their tails, keeping a mist of water all around them.

"How are we moving?" Elise asked Meallán. He shrugged.

Laisrén overheard her question and grinned. "Magic," he whispered with a smirk.

The green Adaro, by far the chattiest of the bunch, overheard him and snorted. "Don't you know anything?" he demanded. "The sunlight hits the water droplets and is refracted to form a visible spectrum of light, commonly called a rainbow."

Elise blinked in surprise. She had wanted something to make sense but hadn't expected it to come from a fish-man who was helping her travel by rainbow.

The Adaro continued, "The Adaros are able to use the visible spectrum to travel outside of our normal aqueous habitat. Our physiology interacts with light as if it was solid. Anything we bring with us, to a certain extent, is able to interact with our auras in a way that transfers our physical characteristics of light travel to them as long as they are within a specific range. Didn't you learn anything in school?" he finished with a snort.

She shook her head. Perhaps she would just stick with magic. She wasn't sure what her science teacher would make of the second half of that explanation.

Not long after the Adaro's explanation ended, Elise noticed that they seemed to be slowing.

"We're losing sunlight," growled Corc. "Someone needs to take care of this problem," he muttered. "These mountains are the worst place lately." He pointed to the dark, hazy mountains shimmering up ahead. "The sun positively refuses to shine anywhere near them."

Meallán nodded. "Don't take us any farther than is safe for you," he said to the Adaros. They erupted in complaints.

"The next thing you know, he'll be telling us that rainbow is a rubbish way to travel," complained the catfish Adaro.

"You might as well say we are incompetent," said the rainbow trout. "No gratitude, these Leprechauns."

A few minutes later, there was a slight tremor and then a few large bumps. "End of the line," shouted Corc. "The sunlight is fading since you managed to show up in the late afternoon when travel is hardest."

"It's going to be a quick exit," grumped the catfish Adaro. "It's too dangerous to stop without any water nearby. We'd never get a rainbow going here, and we'd end up parched and withered in the dry air."

There was a larger bump, and the Adaros swung around and flipped their tails faster, making a rainbow curve down to the forest.

"No doubt everyone around knows you are here now, and your chance at surprise is ruined," grumbled the green one. "Then you'll be blaming us if your quest fails."

"Thank you," Elise shouted as they started to slide away. "That was the best trip ever!"

The Adaros managed to look pleased despite their scowls. They waved and then turned and disappeared back into the air. Despite their complaints that everyone would know they had arrived, Elise couldn't see them traveling through the air at all. Perhaps no one had noticed the brief rainbow that was fading out behind them.

They landed softly on the ground, and Meallán smiled proudly. "They are gruff and can be quite rude, but you have to admit, they get you where you want to go!"

Laisrén snorted. "They are ridiculous."

"But here we are," added Meallán, waving at the dark mountains just ahead of them. "They seemed to think that Murtagh was nearby, and it is likely that there are caves under the mountains. They would make a defensible position and would make any rescue attempt extremely difficult. That would also explain why the queen hasn't been able to escape," he added. He turned to Elise to explain. "Elf magic doesn't work well underground. The longer they are underground, the worse it gets."

"Then let's catch a Pixie!" said Tíreachán. "They've been all over here recently," he added with a big sneeze.

"How do you know that?" asked Laisrén.

"I'm allergic," he admitted with a grin, his face turning a bit pink. "Any Pixie dust makes me sneeze."

"Can you tell where it is strongest?" Meallán asked. "It would be helpful it we knew which direction to go."

"I'll walk around a bit and see where I start sneezing most," offered Tíreachán sarcastically.

"Do you think that will work?" Elise asked in surprise.

Tír gave her a sour look but shrugged and started walking around the clearing. Laisrén snickered but went with him in case he was overcome with sneezing.

"I'll take Amos and see what he can find," said Meallán. "He was able to smell the magic on the stone in the shop, so he might be able to track down a Pixie." Elise watched the two of them walk off together. Amos was ending up with a lot of handy traits that she had never considered before. She felt a bit helpless watching everyone else work.

The others soon came back. Amos was trotting proudly, so Elise guessed he had been able to find the trail of some Pixies. Tíreachán looked a bit red, and his eyes were watering. "We found where they had been gathered," he wheezed. "Amos should be able to carry on from there."

Amos sniffed and managed to look insulted. "He will," replied Elise.

"Now," said Laisrén firmly, "you need to know exactly what to say to the Pixie, or it will give you sketchy dust." Elise sat down to listen. She didn't want to mess this up. "The first thing to remember is that you have to wait until the Pixie feels very threatened. If it thinks it could have escaped by itself it won't really help you, it will just play a prank. If it really feels like you saved it, then it is bound by magic law to give you a gift—pixie dust. When it offers you the dust, ask what it can do. The Pixie will have to explain, and then, you tell it exactly what you want the dust to do. It will be easiest if you say you want dust that will take you wherever you want to go. If it seems suspicious, try to convince it you are just a muddle-headed human who wants to see a unicorn or something silly."

"Are there really unicorns?" Elise asked.

"Stay focused," Laisrén ordered.

Elise grinned and nodded, trying to remember everything Laisrén was saying. It didn't seem too complicated as long as Amos managed to catch one. "What will happen if it is suspicious of me?" she asked.

"Who knows," replied Laisrén with a shrug. "They are tricky and usually travel in a swarm. They like being horrible to everyone, but especially to humans. Mostly because humans don't know anything about them," he said as Tír poked him and looked at Elise with concern. "They almost never do anything too drastic," he finished lamely.

Elise bit her lip and reached for Amos. Suddenly, this didn't seem so harmless.

Meallán smiled reassuringly. "I've given Amos some advice on how to catch one without hurting it. The others will make fun of another

Pixie for getting caught, but if you really hurt one, they will gang up on you." He grinned. "That's when Pixies are really dangerous."

Elise gulped and wiped her suddenly-sweaty palms on her jeans. She was becoming less and less sure about this plan. Her stomach knotted up, but she took a few deep breaths. She had promised to help, and she would. This was also the fastest way to get back home

"Let's get started, then," she said weakly. "Ready, Amos?" she asked, petting his soft head.

He barked and trotted off across the clearing.

"We will be out of sight, but if you need us, just shout," said Tír. "We will be ready."

Elise nodded and followed Amos into the trees.

* * * * *

They had been walking for about ten minutes when Amos came to a stop. He looked at Elise and gave a low growl. She stopped. They must be close. She would have to let Amos go ahead and catch the Pixie before she could come out. She knelt and stroked his long ears.

"Ready for this, Amos?" she asked. "It's not too late to back out."

He licked her hand and trotted off into the trees. *He's not the one who is worried*, Elise thought as she followed him, keeping well back. They would have to be convincing. If Pixies were used to tricking people, they were probably not going to be easily tricked. Soon, she heard Amos bark, followed by the chatter of shrill voices. She couldn't make out what they were saying, but they were definitely unhappy.

She crept forward and peeked through the leaves. Amos was crouched at the far edge of a clearing, sniffing at something trapped between his paws. Elise waited until she saw his tail wagging. He must have one. She took a deep breath and rushed into the clearing. "What have you done?" she shouted. "What do you have there?"

Trapped under Amos's paws was a tiny female creature. She was smaller than Laisrén, but her face was almost catlike. She shouted at Elise with a shrill voice. "Get this monster off of me! What do you mean letting this beast loose in the forest?"

Elise reached for the Pixie but, to her surprise, Amos growled at her and put his head over the Pixie. Elise was shocked. Amos had never growled at her for real. Then, she noticed his tail was still wagging. She glared at him. Traveling with the Faerie had made him even more mischievous. Well, it would make the drama more realistic. She shook her finger at him. "Bad dog," she said sternly. "You know better than to growl at me. I'm going to take that creature from you before you eat it."

Amos licked his lips and let a string of drool fall on the Pixie.

"Don't let it eat me!" a muffled voice shrieked from beneath Amos's head. "Save me!"

In the trees, Elise could hear the shrieks of the other Pixies. She had to stop this before the others got angry at her. She poked Amos, and he lifted his head, growling once more for good measure. The Pixie shrieked again, and Elise grabbed it away from Amos as he pretended to snap at it. Elise felt a moment of pity until the Pixie stood up and started shouting insults at Amos. "It's okay," she said hurriedly. "I've got you now, and I won't let him hurt you."

The Pixie tipped her head, staring at Elise. "Thank you, human," she finally said. "In appreciation for your assistance, I offer you this pinch of Pixie dust." The creature took a small bag from one of her tiny pockets. It would be no more than a pinch, but Elise guessed that it would be enough.

"What does it do?" she asked, carefully remembering all of Laisrén's instructions.

The Pixie looked at her suspiciously but then stuck her lip out in a sullen pout. "It can do whatever you want. It can take you places or bring something to you, and, of course, it can make you fly," she explained as her friends jeered from the trees.

Apparently, it was even worse if the person you had to reward was smart enough or lucky enough to ask for instructions. "It has to be set, so tell me what you want it to do, and I will make it so."

Elise tried to look like she was thinking carefully. "Can it take me anywhere?" she asked. "I'm trying to find my way home, but I don't know where to go." She tried to sound confused, like a lost human might. She felt tears pricking her eyes and blinked. This wasn't the time to think about how true that statement was. It must have convinced the Pixie, though, because she smirked a bit.

"It can take you anywhere in the Faerie Realm," said the Pixie, "but there's not enough to get you to the Human Realm." She smiled, but the catlike grin was not very nice.

"Oh!" exclaimed Elise with her eyes opened as big as she could manage. "I'm not sure where I want to go then. Can you make it take me wherever I tell it to go? That way when I decide where to go, I can get there!" she exclaimed, looking carefully at the Pixie, who looked suspicious but then shrugged in resignation.

"Fine," she said as the Pixies above laughed. "But you have to give clear directions."

"That would be wonderful!" Elise gasped.

The Pixie mumbled into the bag and shook it sharply. "That will do it," she said. "It will take you wherever you want to go."

"Thank you!" said Elise as the Pixie dropped the bag in her hand and hovered in front of her. "How does it work?" she asked. "Do I have to say something to make it work?"

There was more jeering from the trees. The Pixie laughed wickedly. "Not a thing. Just think about where you want to go and sprinkle it into the air."

"Thank you," Elise said again as the Pixie flew away. She called Amos and hurried back to find the others.

Tír sighed with relief when he saw them. "I'm glad that worked," he said. "There are so many things that can go wrong when you're dealing with Pixies."

"And we forgot to tell you that the Pixie was free of its obligation when you said thank you. If it gives you your reward and is set free, it doesn't have to tell the truth anymore. If you had said it too soon, who knows what might have happened," Laisrén said with a smirk. Elise glared at him. There didn't seem to be much difference between Pixies and Fairies sometimes.

"Laisrén was taking bets that one of you would end up charmed," added Meallán with a grin. "He owes me a spell." Laisrén made a face at Meallán but smiled innocently at Elise.

"But where should we go?" asked Elise. "If we tell the dust to take us to the princess, we could end up locked up with her, or the guards will see us, and we'll just get captured too.

"We will have to go to the entrance of Murtagh's hideout," said Tír thoughtfully. "Maybe we can find a way to slip inside and rescue both the princess and the queen."

"I don't like the odds of that plan," said Laisrén. "I don't think we will be able to just walk in."

"Maybe there is a back door," said Elise. "I would think Murtagh would want a back door in case something happened, and he had to get away."

Meallán nodded. "I'm sure there is, and it will probably be less guarded than the front door." He looked at the Pixie dust. "There's only enough there for one trip, so we have to do it right. Everyone, grab hold. Tír, grab Amos. Laisrén, get a spell ready in case there are guards." He looked at Elise. "You need to say exactly where you want to go and then dump the dust out of the bag."

"The Pixie told me I didn't have to say anything," said Elise in confusion. "It said to just think it."

"It lied," said Laisrén cheerfully. "You said thanks before you got to that part. Pixies usually try to get away as quickly as possible, so they can start tricking people again."

Elise rolled her eyes at his cheerful tone but looked at the small bag of dust and thought for a moment. "I want to go to the back entrance of Murtagh's hideout—the one where he has the princess," she added hastily, as she dumped out the dust. There was a small whoosh, and suddenly, they were on the other side of the mountain standing in front of a cave. A river gushed out of the mouth of the cave and flowed down into the valley.

"That went surprisingly well," said Meallán, looking into the cave. "It doesn't look like anyone is guarding this door."

"That went too well," muttered Laisrén. "There have to be guards somewhere. There's no way Murtagh would leave an entrance unguarded." He pulled out his wand and flew into the cave. After a moment, he came back. "I don't trust this, but it seems you are right," he said to the Leprechaun. "There is no one here."

"No one is here *now*," corrected Tír. "We need to be ready for anything."

Elise looked at the cave. The river filled most of the opening, leaving just enough room for a narrow path curling around the edge of the rock. If anyone slipped off the path, the river would sweep them away in an instant. Elise shivered. "What do we do?" she asked.

Tír looked at the cave and then at the rest of them. "I think Amos and Meallán should stay here. Meallán is too recognizable unless he makes himself invisible the whole time. I don't think any Leprechauns have joined Murtagh. Amos will have a hard time on the path, and we need someone on the outside in case we run into trouble. I can blend in with the other Gruagacha here, and maybe we can disguise Elise as a small giant." Elise giggled. She was beginning to enjoy being considered a giant. "Laisrén should be able to fly high enough to stay out of sight."

"But what do we do when we get in there?" asked Laisrén. "We have no idea where to look."

"We'll just have to search the best we can and hope no one notices us," replied Tír. Elise put on her jacket and looked through her backpack for a hat. No one had anything else that would fit her, however, so that was the extent of her disguise.

Laisrén snorted as he watched Elise's preparations. "That's your plan? Wander around in Murtagh's hideout and hope we find their two most valuable prisoners? That's going to be simple. What could go wrong?" He fluttered in front of Tír. "What do we do if someone sees us?"

"Magic," Tír snapped back at him. "You can do that, right?" He threw his hands in the air. "What else can we do? We have no information about what we will find inside. We are running out of time. If

Murtagh takes over the kingdom, we are all in trouble. If he loses, my mother may be put on trial for treason. We have to stop this now!"

Amos growled and snapped at Laisrén, who dodged out of the way. "Fine," he said, "we will do it your way. But if you get captured, I'm not going to risk my wings to come rescue you."

"Fair enough," said Meallán calmly, in the same voice he used with the Adaros. He looked at Tír with the same strange look on his face that Elise had seen before. "I'm sorry," he blurted out.

"What?" Tír stopped, confused.

"I'm sorry," Meallán said again. "For telling everyone you got caught in the kitchen that night. Anyway," he continued, as everyone turned to stare at him, "perhaps we should get started? As you mentioned, we don't know how much time we have before Murtagh attacks the castle."

Tír nodded silently and loosened his sword.

Amos licked Elise's hand, and she had a moment of panic at the thought of leaving him. "What do I do if someone realizes I'm human?" she asked, sitting down for a moment to hug Amos and take a few deep breaths. "I don't have any magic, and I can't blend in."

"You're a lot bigger than everyone else so just shove them out of the way and run," suggested Meallán.

Elise made a face but nodded. It wasn't great, but that was probably the best idea for her.

They crept into the cave, and Laisrén pulled out his wand. A blue light glowed around them as they edged along the slippery path. A few yards into the cave, the path widened into a sandy riverbank, and they saw another tunnel leading into the mountain.

"This must be it," said Tír. "Try to stay together. If we get separated, find your way back here."

They tiptoed into the tunnel, listening for anything that would give them a hint about what they were getting themselves into. As the light from the entrance faded, Elise dug through her backpack for her flashlight. Soon, they saw the flicker of light ahead. Laisrén flew ahead to look. Suddenly, there was a shout and angry voices echoed down the tunnel.

"Laisrén must have been seen," Tír whispered to Elise. "Stay here while I go see if I can find out what is going on."

Elise tried to protest, but before she could say anything, Tír had slipped away. Elise looked around at the black walls and felt the familiar feeling of panic building in her stomach. She sat down and tried to focus, but her thoughts were interrupted by the sound of tramping footsteps coming from behind her. They would discover her in seconds. "I hope Laisrén is the kind of Fairy who can grant wishes," Elise said under her breath. "I wish you would come find me," she whispered as she crept down the hallway. She managed a small smile imagining what Laisrén would say if he knew she had made a wish for him to grant.

Caught between the brightly-lit room ahead and the footsteps behind, Elise turned down the next tunnel she found. A flight of steep steps ended at an intersection. She breathed a sigh of relief as the footsteps passed by and faded, but then jumped and let out a little squeak as something brushed her arm in the dark. Panicked, she ran down one of the tunnels. Every time she thought she was safe, a falling rock or the sound of voices set her running again. Finally, she stopped, crying with fear, in a large open room. She was lost.

Being lost was one of her many fears, so she and Aunt Mim had talked through things to do if that ever happened. Elise mentally reviewed her list of steps but found that none of them seemed very helpful in this case. *Look for a familiar landmark*. There were no landmarks here. Nothing had been familiar since she had fallen into the Faerie Realm. *Find a police officer or someone to help*. Anyone she found here was unlikely to help her. They were more likely to lock her up with the princess and queen. Then, someone would have to come rescue her. *Stay where you are and wait for someone to find you*. If she stayed, someone would very likely find her, but the result would be the same. She had to either hide or find her way out by herself.

Tír walked down the passageway, trying to look like he belonged here. In one way, he did, he realized with surprise. If Murtagh hadn't chosen to kidnap the princess and the queen, Tír might have been tempted to support him.

The passageway ended in a brightly-lit room. Tír saw that the shouting hadn't been because of Laisrén, but because there was some disagreement happening between Murtagh and the Gruagacha following him.

"Prisoners or not," one Gruagacha was saying, "King Brian is not going to just hand over the throne. We will have to fight, and we are no match for the Gnome army. You have to do something about them before we try to take the castle."

"Impossible," said Murtagh. "Even with the queen's power, it will take too much energy to deal with the whole Gnome army at once. It will leave me too weak once I get inside." He looked around at the Gruagacha in the room. "You want freedom, but you aren't willing to fight for it?" he asked with a sneer. "This is why you are still the slaves of the Elves. This is why it took someone like me to make all this happen."

"Perhaps," said another older Gruagacha. "But perhaps telling the Elves you are a Gruagacha who could do magic would have had the same result. No one could deny that you are very powerful. You could have taught others and peacefully shown the Elves that we have magic. You could still teach us," he said.

Tír watched Murtagh carefully. That argument made a lot of sense. With an army trained to use magic, Murtagh would be a strong threat even without the queen.

Murtagh frowned at the old Gruagacha. "What use would it be to teach you all magic now?" he demanded. "I need soldiers, not magicians. I have enough power myself to overthrow King Brian!"

The old Gruagacha shook his head. "Then what have we gained by following you?" he asked simply. "You are different than you were before, Murtagh. I followed you the first time to fight for our people's freedom. This is no longer about the Gruagacha but about revenge on the Elves."

"Then you can join the queen in the dungeon," shouted Murtagh. He turned to the Phooka standing beside him. "Take him to the cellars and lock him up. Anyone else afraid to fight for your freedom?" he shouted to the crowd.

"No!" shouted the first Gruagacha. "We will fight!"

The rest of the Gruagacha followed his lead, and soon, the whole room was shouting in support of Murtagh. Tír pushed his way through the crowd to follow the unfortunate Gruagacha down to the dungeons. He might be able to persuade him to become an ally. He paused as the Phooka neared another room, this one lit by only a single candle. The dim light showed a number of doors set into the rock walls. There was a table in the room, but the two Gruagacha guards were standing outside the entrance. Tír noticed that the Phooka had a ring of keys on a belt slung across one shoulder. Murtagh must not trust the Gruagacha enough to let them guard the queen by themselves.

Tír waited as the Phooka threw the old Gruagacha into a cell and locked the door. He took the keys with him, but Tír let him go. First, he needed to find out if the queen was here.

"What did he do to get thrown in here, I wonder," whispered the first guard, glancing nervously at the retreating Phooka.

"Probably arguing with Murtagh again," said the second. "It was only a matter of time before he lost patience with those who are too afraid to fight. What do people expect, joining an army like this?" He shook his head. "The king has had plenty of time to change his mind. There is no way now except to fight."

"Fighting is one thing," said the first guard. "I don't like this kidnapping and stealing magic. Hiding in this mountain isn't how I pictured the rebellion going."

"We'll go soon enough," said the second guard. "It's got to be soon. The queen won't have much power left if she spends too much longer down here." He glanced back into the room and Tír's heart leaped. The queen must be here. He turned back up the passageway. He needed to find Laisrén and Elise and make a plan.

He met Laisrén halfway up the passageway. "Elise is gone," Laisrén said. "I went back so we could follow you, but she wasn't there."

Tír frowned. This made things more complicated. "I think I've found the queen and the princess," he said, "but I need your help getting passed the two guards. Once we've found her, you go look for Elise, and I'll get them out, and we will meet back at the river."

"What if I can't find her?" asked Laisrén. "There are tunnels all over, and she could be anywhere!"

"We will have to try," said Tír. "Once I get the others out, I will come back and help you look."

"Let's worry about one thing at once," grumbled Laisrén. "First, we need to make sure we have actually found them."

They made their way back down the passage, and Laisrén cast a spell that put the two guards to sleep. "See?" Laisrén mumbled. "Magic. Fixes everything here."

Tír ignored him and started knocking on the doors. "Your Majesty?" he called. "Are you here?"

"I am here," came a voice from behind one of the doors. "Who are you?"

"It's the queen," Tír whispered to Laisrén. "Try to open the door."

Laisrén waved his wand, but the blue light just sparked off the lock. "It's got some kind of spell on it," said Laisrén. "I might be able to break it open, but that would make more of a bang than we really want right now. Stealing the keys might be easier."

Tír nodded. "Go back and find Elise. Meet me at the river, and we will regroup and make a plan. Taking on a Phooka to get the keys won't be quiet, so we should all be together when we try it." He watched Laisrén fly away and hoped he could find Elise.

* * * * *

Elise shined her light around the room. There were doors along each wall but no other tunnel. Maybe she could find a place to hide in one of the rooms. The first few were unlocked and looked to be storage rooms. There was no place to hide in any of them. When she came to one that was locked, she knocked softly on it. She cringed as she imagined Laisrén's sarcastic voice asking if she thought someone might open the door for her, but she didn't know what else to do. The next door was locked, so she knocked on that one as well. Unexpectedly, on the fourth locked door, there was a response.

"Hello?" a voice called softly. "Is someone there?"

"Who are you?" asked Elise in surprise. She hadn't actually expected anyone to answer.

"I am Princess Líoch," the voice said.

"Prince Rauri's princess?" Elise asked in surprise. "We are here to rescue you!"

"Is Rauri here?" The princess's voice quivered with sudden hope.

"No, but he is back in the Faerie Realm," answered Elise. "Let me see if I can get you out." She looked around. "Do you know where the keys are?"

"I do not," answered the princess. "I was not awake when they put me in here, and I have not been out since. I do not even know where I am."

"I don't really know either," confessed Elise. "You're under a mountain near a river. That's really all I know." She looked back at the doorway and sighed. "I'm here with some other people. I'll try to find them and see if we can get you out."

She hurried back to the tunnel, wondering how she was going to find the others and then get back here when she didn't even know where here was. As she started down the tunnel, she froze in horror as a light appeared, flickering on the wall. Someone was coming. Covering her flashlight, except for the smallest beam, she ran back to the room, slipped through one of the open doors, and waited. If it was someone with the keys, maybe she could get them.

As the light passed, Elise saw a single Gruagacha carrying a plate of food. She hesitated. She didn't know anything about fighting and wasn't sure what she could do. The guard would have a sword. Elise shook her head, remembering Meallán's advice. Maybe she could just push him into the princess's room. She was a lot bigger than he was.

She slowly pushed the door open and peeked along the wall. The guard set down the plate and pounded on the door. "Back up, princess," he commanded. "When I open the door, you'd better be against the wall where I can see you." He waited a moment and then unlocked the door and pushed it open without stepping inside. Apparently, the princess had obeyed because he picked up the food and bent down to set it inside the door. Without stopping to think, Elise dashed from her hiding place and pushed him as hard as she could. Off balance, the guard fell over into the room, hitting his head on the solid wooden door.

"Come on!" shouted Elise.

The princess dodged the guard, who lay dazed on the floor, his hands holding his head. Elise shoved his feet out of the way and managed to get the door closed. The guard had left the key in the lock. She turned the key and put it in her pocket.

"This way," she said as she grabbed the princess's hand and ran down the tunnel.

"Where are we going?" the princess asked.

"I'm not sure," admitted Elise. "I'm actually lost."

"Well, we cannot stay here," said the princess logically. "Let us look for the tunnel that seems to be the most used." They looked at each other and smiled a little. It wasn't so bad being lost when you were with someone else. The sound of footsteps wiped the smiles from their faces.

"Hide," gasped Elise. They ran back and ducked into one of the side tunnels. Another Gruagacha passed carrying a bucket.

"There are too many Gruagacha around," whispered the princess. "He will be taking that down to my cell. We have to find a way out now before they realize I have escaped."

"Maybe not," said Elise thoughtfully. "If they know you have escaped, they will try to stop you from getting away from the caves. They will check the quickest way out first. I read something like this in a book once. We can just follow them to the exit and get out."

"Wait," said the princess. "My mother is here, too. We have to try to find her."

Elise shook her head. "We can't wander around for long without getting caught. Maybe the others found her and will meet us by the river. Once we find the way out, we can decide what to do next." They waited until the Gruagacha came running back, followed by the one Elise had pushed into the room. The two girls struggled to keep up without getting too close.

Soon, the two men stopped. "You check the back door while I go tell Murtagh what happened," growled the second man. "You'd better hope you catch them or you've had it."

"It wasn't my fault," complained the first man. "How was I supposed to know they had a giant hiding in the storerooms?"

"Stop whining and get her back," ordered the second man.

The girls looked at each other and followed the first man toward the exit. He hurried down the tunnel, stopping now and then to look into the side passages suspiciously. Finally, Elise heard the sound of the river. She squeezed the princess's hand, and they ducked into one of the side passages.

"What should we do?" asked the princess. "How will we get out with him waiting there."

"Well, in the book, the man was invisible and just jumped over the person he was following," admitted Elise. "But we should be able to get past one guard. Can you do magic?" she asked hopefully.

"Some," said the princess. "But I have been deep underground since Murtagh had the bracer on me, and that is not good for our magic. I am not sure how much I can manage."

"Maybe you can distract him, and I can push him down again," suggested Elise. "If we can get outside, Amos will take care of him." She looked down the tunnel, wishing she was already out in the fresh air and light.

"Ready?" she whispered to the princess.

"Ready," Princess Líoch whispered.

Princess Líoch stepped through the entrance into the cave. Elise heard the Gruagacha laugh. She peeked around the doorway to watch for her chance.

"You were too slow, princess," he said. "Now, where is your friend? I'll take care of that giant and get you back to your cell before Murtagh has the chance to get angry."

"There was no giant," the princess said primly. "Even under this great mountain, my magic was more than enough to take care of you." She held out her hands and said, "Vilagíto."

The man jumped back but laughed again. "You've been underground far too long, princess." He began to circle around to block Líoch's escape down the path. "There is no way out," he said in a grating voice. "Just come back, and we can forget this whole thing ever happened."

Líoch raised her hands and shouted, "Vilagíto!" A flash of light filled the room, and the man cried out and covered his eyes. Elise, blinking away spots from her vision, ran into the cave and pushed the man as hard as she could. He staggered a few steps and then fell into the river with a sharp cry.

"Well done, Elise," the princess said weakly. "Now what? That was the last of my magic until I have some time to recover."

A blue light flickered in the tunnel. Elise gasped and pulled the princess behind some rocks. The light flitted into the cave. "Laisrén? Is that you?" she asked.

"Elise?" Laisrén hovered, staring at Elise. "Where have you been? I came back to get you, but you had gone. I've been looking all over for you. What was that light?"

"Um, I found the princess," she said, pulling the Elf from behind the rock.

Laisrén froze and then caught himself as he started to fall. "Uh, hi, Your Highness," he said. He turned to Elise. "Tír found out where the queen is and is trying to get her out. He sent me to find you. Get the princess out, and I'll go see if I can find him." He shook his head as he turned back toward the tunnel. "This is the poorest planning of any rescue mission ever," he muttered.

"I am Tíreachán," Tír finally answered the queen, "a Gruagacha who serves Prince Rauri. We are here to rescue you."

"Prince Rauri is here?" the queen asked, her voice lifting with sudden hope.

"Well, no," admitted Tír. "We think he is trapped in the castle. But we are here to rescue you nevertheless."

"Who is with you?" asked the queen.

"A Fairy, a Leprechaun, a human girl who helped us return home, and her faithful hound," answered Tír, hoping he didn't sound as foolish as he felt.

"An unusual troupe," said the queen, "but you seem to have found success so far." She paused for a moment and then asked, "Why do you not follow Murtagh? Are you content with your position in life?"

"No," admitted Tír. "But fighting isn't the way to change things. This realm belongs to all of us, and starting a war now, even if we feel we are in the right, will only hurt us all in the end." He hesitated. "Although Murtagh has proven that our claims are just," he continued with a rush. "He is a Gruagacha, but he has learned to use magic. Surely, that proves that the Gruagacha have the same magic as the Elves."

"Then the rumors were true," said the queen in astonishment. "We had heard this but did not believe it. Why did he not simply show his magical ability and prove his power?"

Tír didn't answer. He didn't know how to explain to the queen that none of the Gruagacha really trusted the Elves to admit they were wrong. Somehow, they always made it the Gruagacha's fault.

"How do you know this?" the queen asked, as the silence lengthened.

"Well, he's my uncle," Tír admitted. "My mother told me just before she was arrested by the army. She could do magic, too, so I guess it must run in our family."

"In that case," the queen said, "perhaps you would be willing to try some magic here. If I do magic, Murtagh will know. The bracers connect our power, and he will feel me working. But I can teach you the words you need to open the doors and to get us out. If the king is arresting Gruagacha, then they will be all the more willing to follow Murtagh, and war will be upon us soon."

"Where is the princess?" Tír asked suddenly. In his conversation with the queen, he had forgotten her.

"I do not know," said the queen. Her voice was both sad and angry at the same time. "Murtagh separated us and threatened that if I tried to do any magic, he would have her killed. I would do anything to keep Murtagh from overthrowing the kingdom, but I must be certain of success before I would make that sacrifice."

"Well, let's do one thing at a time," said Tír. "Maybe we can see who else is down here and get some more help."

"Listen carefully, then," said the queen. "I am going to teach you a word that will crumble the stone of the wall. You must say the word I will teach you and focus on the area around the lock. It may help, at first, to touch the stone as well. You are telling it what to do, but you must also picture it happening." She paused. "I do not know how powerful you are, so start by focusing a bit of the power you feel. Do not use it all. If there is not enough effect, you can always do it again. Say the word *elmorzsol* and then close your hand. Let me stand back before you try," she finished with a small laugh.

Tír swallowed and thought the word in his mind as he touched the stone wall. He jumped as he felt a sharp crackling power that seemed to spark in his hand. *That must be what the queen was talking about*, he thought. Just a little. "Here goes," he said. "Elmorzsol." He closed his hand and imagined the stone around the lock crumbling.

He heard a deep rumble, and his eyes popped open just as a large section of the wall crumbled into pebbles. When the dust cleared, he saw two faces staring at him. One was the queen, and the other was the old Gruagacha who had refused to fight.

"Well," said the Gruagacha, "that was an eye-opener and no doubt!"

"Was that just a little of your power?" asked the queen, raising one eyebrow.

Tír nodded, unsure that his voice would work.

The queen smiled. "Then you are going to be quite a surprise for Murtagh." She looked at the old Gruagacha. "What are your intentions?"

"I'm going to get out of here and wait for this youngster to prove me right," the old Gruagacha said with a grin. "I always said if we could get one powerful Gruagacha, the Elves would have to listen." He looked at Tír proudly. "And here you've saved the queen! There's no going back now." He bowed to Queen Keeva and then, to Tír's surprise, bowed to him as well, before trotting up the passageway and out of sight.

"He is right, you know," said the queen, looking at Tír carefully. "This is going to change everything. You may not need to fight to prove you are equal to the Elves. You are the proof and, whether he wants it or not, so is Murtagh if you can get the right people to listen. Now," she said briskly, "we will need a few more words in order to make our escape."

"Wait," said Tír. "We should try to take the bracer off."

"Once you are ready to fight," said the queen. "I am afraid Murtagh will know once I remove it, and then we will lose our element of surprise."

Tír nodded and focused on the words the queen taught him. There were only two, but the queen assured him they would be enough. "One puts people to sleep, and the other is a blinding flash of light. No one is expecting any magic, so that alone will get us through most of the people here. Until you have learned to control

138

your power, these are the safest words to learn. Now," she said, "you must try to remove the bracer. I cannot."

Tír reached out, but as soon as he touched the bracer, a shock of power knocked him backward.

"Enough," the queen said. "I was afraid that once it was put on by magical means, it would prove difficult to remove. We shall try again when we have found the princess."

They stole up the passage to the large room. There were not as many Gruagacha as before, but Tír still looked nervously at the crowded room.

"Focus," said the queen. "Speak the word and spread your hand across the room. Use only a little power. Conserve your strength."

Tír spread his hand and waved it across the room. "Alvás." Immediately, all the Gruagacha tumbled to the floor. He looked around with awe.

"Well done," said the queen. "Lead on."

Tír led the queen across the room toward the passage to the river.

They made it nearly halfway across the room when someone shouted, "It's the queen! Someone stop her!"

The queen spoke a word, and they were suddenly plunged into darkness. With another word, the queen held a small ball of light. As they ran into the tunnel, Tír heard shouting from different passageways as more Gruagacha poured in to find out what was happening.

"Hurry!" said the queen. "Using my magic will help Murtagh find us more easily."

They raced down the passage. Tír hoped that Laisrén had found Elise. He turned and spoke the other word the queen had taught him. A bright light flashed through the darkness of the tunnel. The shadows of the following Gruagacha scattered in confusion.

They ran on toward the river.

* * * * *

Elise and Princess Líoch watched as Laisrén flew into the tunnel. Almost immediately, he flew back in.

"Hide!" he shouted.

He was followed by a burst of light, and Tír rushed out of the tunnel holding on to the queen's arm.

"Mother!" the princess shrieked.

"That was some flashy magic, Your Majesty," said Laisrén, impressed.

"That was not me," said the queen. "That was your friend. It seems he has powerful magic once he learns the proper words."

"You can do magic, too?" shouted Laisrén. "Your mother, your crazy uncle, and now you. Why can suddenly every Gruagacha do magic?"

"Shh," hissed Tír. "There were a bunch of Gruagacha right behind us. We don't have much time before they get here."

"I taught him," said the queen, answering Laisrén's question. "It seemed the most straightforward way of getting out." She held up her arm, which was encased in the magic bracer. "With this on, my magic is very limited." She looked at Tír with pride. "It seems we have been wrong about the Gruagacha. You are nearly as powerful as me."

Everyone stared at Tír, who was left speechless at the queen's revelation.

The queen hugged her daughter and smiled. "We should be going," she reminded them. Before they could move, a man walked out of the tunnel.

"Quick," whispered the princess, "get the bracer off." She grabbed her mother's arm but immediately snatched her hand away, crying out in pain.

The man laughed. "It is not that simple, Your Highness. The bracer cannot be removed by any magic except that which put it on." He smiled and held up his arm. "I wear the other bracer, so I alone can remove it."

"Murtagh," said the queen, "I demand that you let us go at once."

Murtagh laughed again as his soldiers came running out of the tunnel. "You are in no position to make demands, Your Majesty. In fact, I am here to make one of you. You will come with me now to convince the king to turn over his throne to someone who deserves it, and I will let your daughter live."

The queen looked at the Gruagacha, who were all holding arrows pointed straight at the group. "But you are forgetting one thing, Murtagh," she said grimly. "We are no longer far from the outside. There is fresh air here. And water." She raised her hands.

"You can't defeat all of us," Murtagh said. "Any magical battle will be doubly draining for you. You cannot win."

"I do not need to win," whispered the queen. She looked at her daughter and shouted, "Dobás!" She flung one hand back. Immediately, Elise felt herself fly through the air and land in the river.

The princess cried out as she and Tír landed next to Elise. They came up just in time to see Queen Keeva fling her other hand forward, shouting, "Huzat!"

The current carried them down the river, and they were outside the mountain before they could see what happened to the queen. Amos started barking as they were carried past. They fought their way to the edge of the river and pulled themselves onto the bank. Laisrén caught up with them a few moments later.

"Why did you not stay with her?" demanded the princess.

"I stayed long enough to hear their plan. I didn't want to get caught," replied the Fairy. He grinned. "Besides, I didn't want to get in your mother's way. Murtagh is lucky she has been underground for the past few days. She is really something!"

They looked back at the mountain but couldn't see the cave any longer. "We have to find Meallán and Amos," said Tír. "And then, we have to figure out how to get back to the castle."

"My mother is still in there," said the princess. "We have to rescue her!"

"They won't be there for long," said Laisrén. "Just after she threw you all into the water, Murtagh managed to catch her again. He is taking her to the castle to convince the king to give up the throne." He looked grim. "She was still wearing the bracer, so he would just drain her magic if she did manage to escape." He looked at the sobbing princess. "Don't worry, princess," he said encouragingly. "Your mother is too valuable. Murtagh won't hurt her."

"He had better not," muttered the princess, wiping a few tears from her cheeks.

There was a crashing in the bushes, and Amos burst out of the forest. He jumped on Elise and licked her face. "I'm fine, Amos," she said with a laugh. Meallán appeared behind Amos, carrying all their packs, and bowed to the princess.

"Your Highness," he said. "I'm glad we found you."

"Thank you," the princess said jumping a little as Amos sniffed her. "We need to get to the castle before Murtagh hurts my mother."

"I don't know how quickly we can get there," said Tír. "He's probably using Pixie dust, and we can't get near a Pixie for anything after we just caught one."

"What about the Adaros?" Elise asked. "Is there a way to call them? They could get us there fast."

"I'm afraid we can't," said Meallán. "They are often traveling, but none will be around here since it is too dangerous for them."

"Then we start walking," said the princess grimly, "and keep our eyes open for Pixies or another way to get there."

They picked up their bags and started off into the trees.

"Just like you people to walk straight away from the one place we can pick you up out here," shouted a grumpy voice from the river. "Why didn't you say there was a river on this side of the mountain? It would have saved us a lot of trouble."

The group ran back to the river. There, on the bank, sat their four Adaro friends.

"Corc!" shouted Elise. "How did you know we needed you?"

"We got a message from a Naiad that the queen and princess had been seen around here. Took a while for the message to make it through the waterways. As soon as we heard that, we knew you lot would likely be in trouble soon, so we came back and have been keeping watch for you."

The princess took his face in her hands and gave him a big kiss. "This is the best news we could have heard," she said. "Is it true you can get us to the palace quickly?"

Corc was a bit stunned by the unexpected kiss, but the others made up for his silence. "Of course we can," shouted the green Adaro. "Rainbows are the quickest way to get anywhere."

"The others are traveling by Pixie dust," said Tír. "How do your rainbows compare? How far behind will we be?"

The Adaro looked even more offended, if that was possible. "Less far behind if you lot would stop standing around gabbing," one shouted. "Let's get moving. We can discuss details on the way."

They crowded together. The Adaros flicked their tails in the water and then over the company. Elise felt the swooshing feeling of being sucked onto the slide again, and then, they were gliding through the shimmery air.

Rainbows move quickly, but it was clear that they were going to be much slower than the group traveling by Pixie dust. Tír, Meallán, and Laisrén had a chance to talk about their plan. The princess wanted to charge straight into the throne room and start fighting, but Tír shook his head.

"Murtagh still has the bracer on the queen. The longer she is out of the caves, the stronger she will become which means the stronger he will become. We need to find a way to get the bracer off before we attack."

"We'd better hope Murtagh has taken the barrier down, or we might not be able to even get in," added Laisrén.

"He will have to take it down in order to get in," said Meallán. "Besides, he won't care as long as he has the queen."

Elise saw the outlines of Keletvar approaching, shimmering through their watery bubble. They were almost there.

"Look," called Laisrén, pointing below. "The Gnomes are heading toward Keletvar."

They looked down through the trees and saw an army of Gnomes and Elves nearing the city.

"We have to hurry," said Meallán. "The Gnomes aren't going to be happy when they find the Gruagacha in the city."

Keletvar Castle sat in the center of the city. It looked more like a huge house and not like the fairy-tale castle that Elise had imagined. The three wings of the castle made three sides of a rectangle with a thick wall and strong gates making up the fourth side. In the area between the shorter sides of the building, there was an open courtyard where they could see soldiers gathered—Gnomes and Elves near the building and Gruagacha, Pixies, and Phookas waiting outside the gates.

"That doesn't look good," said Meallán. "The Gruagacha have rallied behind Murtagh. King Brian must have made them more upset than he anticipated. Though, when those Gnomes get here, the Gruagacha won't last long."

"We have to stop Murtagh first," said Tír. "Then, maybe, we can stop the Gruagacha before they start a war."

The princess directed the Adaro to drop them off on the roof of the castle. They promised to keep someone passing by just in case they needed a quick getaway. Elise watched in surprise as the princess led them down a short ladder and in through a tall window.

"Not many people know about this entrance," the princess said with a grin. "Hopefully, we can make it down to the throne room before anyone realizes we are in the castle."

They followed the princess, who led them to a curtained balcony above the throne room. They had made it in time, but not by much. The king was arguing with Murtagh, but every time he said something Murtagh didn't like, Murtagh would raise his arm and the queen would get a bit more pale. There was a troupe of Gnomes waiting for the signal from the king to attack. Neala was lurking at the rear of the group, trying to avoid drawing attention to herself. Prince Rauri was standing next to the king, holding his sword but not making any move toward Murtagh.

The princess gasped, but Tír held her back. "We have to act together," he said. "As long as the queen is wearing the bracer, we can't afford to attack Murtagh."

"None of us can take it off," whispered the princess furiously. "How are we supposed to get around his magic?"

"What if I were able to take off the bracer?" Elise asked suddenly. "It's magic, but I don't have any magic, so maybe I can get it off." She hesitated. "If I can't, then at least you'll have a giant and a giant dog to help fight Murtagh. Maybe Amos can get to him before he can do much harm."

Tír looked at the others. They looked doubtful, but it was the best plan they had.

"You'll need a distraction," said Meallán.

"Neala is down there," said Laisrén. "I bet she could create a big distraction."

Tír nodded. "Okay, Elise and the princess will wait until we have surprised Murtagh, and then you will try to get the bracer off the queen. Everyone else," he paused and looked at Laisrén and Meallán with a grin, "wait for Neala's signal and then jump out and start fighting."

Meallán sighed but agreed. "That's not much of a plan, but it will have to do," he said.

The princess nodded. "We will need a few minutes to get downstairs," she said as Laisrén flew off to talk to Neala.

Amos followed them as they made their way downstairs. As they came down the stairs, a Phooka loomed out from a dim hallway. Elise shrieked, and the princess grabbed for something to fight with. Amos growled and lunged at the Phooka. Elise and the princess were trapped on the stairs by the circling combatants.

"We have to get in position," gasped Elise. "They will be starting soon."

They slipped around Amos as he jumped on the Phooka again and ran for the throne room. Just as they were getting into position, there was a shout, and chaos erupted in the throne room.

"That's our signal," Elise said, and she and the princess ran out. Amos bounded past them, barking furiously and snapping at anyone who got in their way. He cleared such a wide space that the girls were able to get to the queen with no trouble. She was pale and lying on the ground. Murtagh was draining her strength as he shouted and threw bolts of magic at Prince Rauri and King Brian. The princess grabbed her mother's wrist but was thrown back by the shock.

"Do not touch it," whispered the queen. "It will take your magic, too."

"Let me try!" ordered Elise. She grabbed the bracer and felt a tingle run up her arms, like an electric shock. It was uncomfortable, but she could stand it. "The knots are too tight," she cried as she pulled at the laces. The princess grabbed a dagger that had fallen nearby and handed it to Elise. She cut through the ties and tore the bracer off the queen's arm.

The queen sighed and lay back. "That is much better," she said with relief.

Murtagh cried out when the queen's bracer was removed, and soon, his power started to falter. He pulled out his sword as Prince Rauri ran toward him.

"Your magic is gone, Murtagh," Prince Rauri said as he faced the Gruagacha. "Surrender."

"I will not," replied Murtagh. "I will fight with or without magic until my people are free."

"Things will change," the prince said. "They must change now."

"There will never be true change while Elves rule," said Murtagh, swinging his sword at the prince.

The prince and Murtagh fought fiercely. The prince was the better swordsman, but Murtagh took advantage of every obstacle to try to trip up his opponent. Finally, the prince struck the sword from Murtagh's hand. He raised his sword for a final blow but stopped.

"You will answer to the king for what you have done," he said.

As Murtagh's followers saw that he had been defeated, they surrendered or disappeared from the hall. The Gnomes followed them, intent on rounding them up.

Neala came over with two soldiers, who grabbed Murtagh's arms. The soldiers brought him to where the king was standing, holding his sword. The king looked to where the queen lay with the princess holding her head. She smiled and gave a small nod.

"What shall we do with you this time, Murtagh?" asked the king. "Before, we banished you for starting a war in our realm. This time, you kidnapped the queen and the princess and have turned many Elves into wraiths. All these crimes should lead to your death."

Murtagh glared up at the king. "What difference does it make?" he demanded. "The Elves have forced my people into servitude for generations. I swore when I was still young that the Elves would pay for the way they treated the Gruagacha. If my death is what it takes to end the rule of the Elves, then I am satisfied."

"Then it is true," said the king. "You are not an Elf but a Gruagacha." He looked thoughtfully at Murtagh. "No," he finally said. "You will not die." Murtagh looked surprised. "You will help to restore the wraiths back to their former selves, and then, you will be banished again. This time to a worse realm and without your followers." He looked coldly at Murtagh. "You will soon see that there are worse existences than what you had here."

Murtagh's defiant expression never changed. "At least I will be free. Do what you will," he replied coldly. "I will never help you."

"You do not have to do it willingly," answered the king. "Remove the bracer from his arm and gather the other. We will see if our magicians can come up with a way to restore the magic that was stolen from the others. Watch him closely. Three men with him at all times and two more outside the door."

As the soldiers took Murtagh away, a soldier came running into the throne room. "Your Majesty," he said, bowing. "There is still an army of Gruagacha outside the gates. What should we do?"

The king looked at Prince Rauri. "Take the rest of the army and remove them," he said angrily. "Use whatever force necessary."

Prince Rauri hesitated and looked at the others. "Perhaps this can be settled without further fighting," he said. "After we have seen that a Gruagacha can indeed perform magic, we must acknowledge that they have reason for their discontent."

"Discontent?" King Brian bellowed. "They supported a traitor who captured your fiancée and my wife, and you think they have a reason for that?"

"They do!" shouted a voice from behind the prince. Tír stepped out and faced the king angrily. "For years, we have been treated like slaves. You have forbidden any Gruagacha from learning the ancient language and made us work while you collected the benefits. Any time we asked for change, you treated us like criminals. Even now, you have arrested my mother, who was trying to convince her neighbors to work for change in peace." He looked angrily around the room. "You all believe we are inferior, but you are wrong. As terrible as Murtagh is, he is proof that we are as capable of magic as you."

The queen rose and walked unsteadily toward the king. "He is right," she admitted. "In the caves, this Gruagacha was capable of very powerful magic, and we have all seen what Murtagh is capable of." She smiled at Tír. "Tíreachán risked his life to rescue me, and he and his friends got our daughter to safety. Let him have his chance to save his people."

The king frowned but nodded. "Keep the gates closed but let him talk to them from the towers. If they do not leave willingly, force them."

Before Tír made it to the door, it burst open again. "Captain Aedan has returned, and the Gruagacha have attacked," the soldier cried. "They are fighting throughout the city."

"No!" cried Tír. "We have to stop them!"

"It will be difficult to stop everyone," said Rauri grimly. "I am afraid we may have to fight our way through and stop each group separately."

"Perhaps not," said the queen. "I can freeze large groups of them momentarily. Long enough to get their attention. After that, they may be willing to listen. Word will travel quickly, especially if we can find someone to quickly take our message to the captain," she said with a pointed look at Laisrén.

"I'm not a Pixie, you know," he grumbled. "I can't just transport myself places. I have to fly there through a battle. I'll be lucky to make it through."

"Will you go?" asked the queen.

"Of course," he answered, pretending to be surprised at her question. "I just wanted you to know how dangerous it is going to be."

The queen smiled. "Tell Captain Aedan that we will try to stop the fighting from the center of the city to the outside. If any Gruagacha retreat peacefully, let them through. If they are still fighting, try to disarm and capture them if possible."

Laisrén bowed and flew away.

"You cannot go," said the king, looking at the queen with concern. "You are not strong enough for that kind of magic."

"Then this Gruagacha can help me," the queen said calmly, but with a twinkle in her eye. "He is very powerful and will be able to stop them much better than I. I will just go along for guidance." She smiled at Tír who paled as he considered the queen's sudden change in plan.

"I don't know if I can do magic like that," he stuttered. "I've never done it before."

"I will help you," said the queen. "But we must hurry. Every moment we delay, more of our people are dying."

"We will come, too," said Neala. "Amos will be a great help in clearing the way. He is excited for the chance to do more to help."

Elise looked at Amos in surprise. Without the Gnomes to translate, she had forgotten how clearly Amos stated his opinions. He looked bored, as usual, but wagged his tail as Neala spoke.

As the group made their way through the castle, the queen taught Tír the word he would need to do his magic. Neala and Amos whispered together, and Elise felt a pang of jealousy that Amos was so excited to be helping Neala. She walked with Meallán and tried not to think about everything that could go wrong.

The Gnome guards snapped to attention and bowed as the group walked through but followed Prince Rauri's command to stay and protect the king and the castle. The area outside the gates was full of Gruagacha. They were strangely silent as they stared through the gates at the waiting Gnome soldiers. As soon as Queen Keeva appeared on the gate tower, a murmur began to ripple through the crowd as they realized Murtagh's rebellion must have been unsuccessful.

"Murtagh has been defeated," Prince Rauri began.

"Down with the Elf oppressors!" someone in the crowd shouted. Immediately, the crowd started shouting and refused to listen, even when the queen raised her hand for silence. Tír looked at the queen then took a deep breath and shouted, "Merev!" Immediately, everyone froze. Elise gasped as she felt her muscles stiffen. For some reason, she had assumed only the crowd would be affected. Everyone's eyes rolled toward Tír as he began to speak.

"Friends, this is not the way to change things," he pleaded. "Murtagh is defeated once again, but this time, our hope is not gone.

Things will change. The queen has helped them see that a Gruagacha can use magic if given the chance to learn. They have seen that we are the same as them. Change may still be slow, but it is not worth the lives that will be lost in this battle. Believe me, Murtagh only wanted power for himself. Despite the fact that he had proof of a Gruagacha's ability to do magic for all these years, he never told anyone. He would have sacrificed all of us to get what he wanted. I know we have been patient our whole lives. I know that many years of oppression have left us desperate for freedom and equality. But change is coming! Help me convince the Elves that we are not what they think we are!"

The crowd listened, and slowly, as the spell faded, they looked around. Some started to drop their weapons. A few at the edge of the crowd slipped away.

"You did it," said Prince Rauri with pride. "They are listening." He slowly moved his arm, stiff from the magic. "And the queen is right. You are quite strong."

Tír looked at the crowd again. "Go home. Put up your weapons and work peacefully for the change that will come."

One of the men bowed slowly to the group on the tower and looked at Tír. "We will wait," he said. "This may indeed be a beginning to the change that we have been looking for. But know this," he looked back at the queen. "We will not wait in peace forever. A change must come, or this will all be repeated." He did not put his sword down but sheathed it and walked back through the crowd. Many of the Gruagacha followed him. A few bowed in the direction of the queen, but Elise thought that, perhaps, they were bowing to Tír as well.

"Well, it's not perfect, but it's better than it might have been," said Neala with a shrug. "Let's move. There is a lot more fighting throughout the city."

Prince Rauri drew his sword as everyone gathered at the gate. "Stay together," he commanded. "Neala, Amos, and I will go first to clear the way. Tír and the queen will come next. Meallán and Elise, you come behind with some of the soldiers and stop anyone from getting to the queen and Tír from behind. Between all of us, we should be able to stop this fighting quickly."

They opened the gate and followed Amos and Neala through the streets. Each time they came upon a group still fighting, Tír would cast his spell and plead with them to put down their weapons. Some Gruagacha surrendered on the spot and were told to leave their weapons and go home. Others left, taking their weapons with them, skeptical, like the first man, that things would truly change. The Gnome soldiers helped by scouting ahead and directing them toward areas of conflict.

As the group made their way through the city, they came upon bands of Gruagacha who were already on their way out. The Gruagacha looked at the queen and Tír with awe. Word was beginning to spread. Finally, on the edge of the city, they met the captain of the Gnome army.

He bowed to the queen. "Welcome back, Your Majesty," he said. "We received your message and have been letting all the peaceful Gruagacha leave the city." He looked at Tír with respect. "They are all in awe of your magic power," he said. "You have given them hope."

"Which makes them even more dangerous," said the prince. "We must change things now, or they will be even more upset."

"Things will change," said the queen calmly. "They cannot help but change sometimes." She turned and looked back at Keletvar. "Poor Murtagh. He fought so hard for this change, but he will not see any of the benefits of it."

"But, strangely, this is still because of him," said Tír. "Despite what he became, he did start out with the idea to help the Gruagacha."

The group made their way back through Keletvar, now filled with cheering townspeople. Elise saw many Elves and Gnomes, but there were also Leprechauns, a few Gruagacha, and a handful of Fairies darting through the air. Meallán was familiar with the city and pointed out different places of interest.

Before, Elise had been too distracted by trying to stop the war to notice much about the city. She looked around with wonder. The roads were cobblestone, well-worn, but kept in good repair. Cheerful wooden houses with colorful shutters lined the streets. The second floor hung out over the first, making them look taller than they really were. Many houses had flowers growing in window boxes. Some larger houses had fenced-in gardens with tidy lawns and neat flower beds that reminded Elise of her garden at home.

The thought made her hurry. There was no way of telling how much time had passed in her world. Aunt Mim and Grams must have been so worried when they woke up and found her gone. She felt sick at the thought of worrying them so much.

Finally, they reached the castle and made their way inside. King Brian had been busy in their absence, and the throne room was back to normal. It was as if the battle there had never happened.

The king welcomed his queen back and quickly sat her on her throne. Once he was sure that she was not overly worn out from her ordeal, he turned to Elise. "Thank you for rescuing my daughter," he said grandly.

Elise blushed. "It was sort of an accident, really," she began. "And I had a lot of help." She pointed to Laisrén, Tír, and Meallán, who were standing nearby. They bowed to the king. Amos barked and bumped Elise with his head. "And Amos," she added.

"What reward can I give you in thanks for my daughter's safe return?" asked the king.

"All I really want," said Elise, "is to get home before I get into any more trouble!" The king smiled. "Aunt Mim will be furious and so worried," Elise continued sadly. "But I can't," she added with a frown. "I ate Faerie food while I was here, and now I can't ever leave."

The king nodded. "It is true that humans who eat Faerie food may not leave the realm by their own means. Therefore, I appoint you the official ambassador from the Faerie Realm to the Human Realm. You must live in the Human Realm and send us word of anything that concerns our kingdom."

Elise beamed. "I would love to, Your Majesty."

"Good," muttered Laisrén. "No one else wants that job."

"The ambassador may need assistance," said the king, glaring at Laisrén. "Perhaps a Fairy assistant?"

Laisrén shook his head in panic.

King Brian turned to the others. "As for the rest of your friends, you will be rewarded for your valiant efforts in stopping the traitor, Murtagh, and restoring peace to our kingdom." He beckoned one of the attendants, who brought an engraved box and offered it to the king. Inside sparkled an array of ruby gems. The king presented one to each of the members of the troupe, including Amos. Neala fastened it onto his collar and whispered something in his ear. Amos sat straight and proud, and Elise rolled her eyes. He was going to be impossible to live with after this.

The king turned back to Elise and Amos. "Go now with our thanks but know that you are always welcome here."

"Yes," agreed the princess, who had been watching the ceremony from beside Prince Rauri. "Please come back for the wedding! We will send word just before. We do not know how long it will be in your world."

"I would love to!" exclaimed Elise.

"You have done a great service to our kingdom," said the queen. "Know that we will always be grateful, and if you ever need help, you have only to call on us."

Elise bowed, thinking that, perhaps, the queen meant more than just saving the princess or helping to defeat Murtagh. The kingdom would be changing in the coming months. The Gruagacha would be waiting for things to change, and now, they had a strong ally in the castle and a Gruagacha hero on their side.

Elise turned to her friends to say goodbye, but Meallán cut her off. "We will go with you back to the passageway," he said. "There are still two Phookas to deal with, and I bet they will be angry!"

"I'd wager they gave up and went back into your realm," said Neala with glee. "Someone will have to go with you and make sure they are taken care of."

"We will all go," said the prince. "We have to check on the others."

"Fergal must be going out of his mind wondering what has been going on," Laisrén said with a smirk. "He will never believe everything that has happened."

Elise prepared herself for another long walk, but the prince motioned a soldier over.

"Bring a squad of soldiers and some traveling powder to the courtyard," he ordered. The man saluted and left the hall. The prince smiled at Elise. "The Pixies trade dust to the Elves instead of money. They give us traveling powder that will take you wherever you want to go."

Elise grinned. She knew all about that powder. They walked to the courtyard. Elise studied the castle as they passed through the halls. It was strangely like walking through her house. She was sad that she wasn't staying any longer, but Aunt Mim and Grams would be so worried. They would have probably called Uncle Jake and everything. She sighed. This wasn't going to be easy to explain. Aunt

Mim would never believe that she had been trapped in the Faerie Realm for the past few days.

They went out the great doors and saw a group of soldiers waiting. Elise saw a few Elves, a lot of Gnomes, and a few Gruagacha mixed in the group. It seemed that Prince Rauri wanted to start making changes immediately. The prince explained their mission, and they all linked arms. He threw a handful of Pixie dust into the air, and suddenly, the whole group was in the clearing in front of the cave.

Laisrén went to check on Fergal and the Brownies in the way station. Neala organized the soldiers to work on clearing the rocks. They had just started when the prince stopped them. He cleared his throat and motioned Tíreachán to come over.

"Perhaps the Gruagacha would like to test their magical strength?" he asked.

Tíreachán nodded. "This is the ideal place," he said with a smile. "If the rocks fall on anyone, it will be a Phooka."

The prince nodded. "Tell the others," he commanded. "It is time we see what the Gruagacha can do."

Tíreachán tried to answer but simply cleared his throat and nodded. He ran over to the group of Gruagacha, and Elise watched as they all listened in amazement.

Meallán smiled. "There's no stopping it now," he said. "King Brian has never made a single change to tradition in his life, but now they have the support of the queen and Prince Rauri, not to mention the Gruagacha who helped stop the war. There has been more change today than the king has ever allowed in all his years on the throne."

In a short time, the rocks had all been removed from the opening. The Gruagacha, tired from the unexpected magic, stepped back to let the Gnomes check the cave. Neala led them in but returned after only a moment. "They aren't there," she reported. "They must have gotten tired of waiting and gone back to the Human Realm."

The prince nodded. "We will send a troupe through to see what they are up to and try to bring them back." He smiled as Neala headed back into the cave. "We will send Neala through first," he said. "Both to make her happy and to make sure there is nothing waiting for you on the other side."

Amos snorted and shook his head. Even Elise understood that.

"It's okay, Amos," she said. "It will make Neala happy. I know you could handle two Phookas with no trouble." She stroked his head.

Behind her, she heard someone clear his throat. She turned to find that Turlach and Branna had joined the group while Fergal and Laisrén had gone to check the cave.

"Goodbye, Elise," Turlach began. "We are very happy to have met you."

Branna threw her arms around Elise and said, "We will miss you very much!"

Meallán laughed and handed Elise a small green stone. "This is a message stone. If you ever need us, just whisper your message in the stone and toss it through the passageway. It will find its way to me," he said.

Tíreachán smiled shyly and held out his hand. "Thank you," he said. "You believed in the Gruagacha and helped start this change."

The prince came over as Tíreachán finished speaking. "Yes," he agreed. "You have brought the beginnings of change to our realm, and we thank you. We will come visit you soon. Watch for us." He bowed to Elise, and she went to the cave to say goodbye to Fergal and Laisrén.

Fergal said a solemn goodbye and promised to see her soon. He also whispered a few words to Amos, who tried to lick the Gnome's face. "Enough of that!" Fergal said sternly.

Laisrén refused to say goodbye just yet. "I'm coming with Neala," he explained. "You are going to be in big trouble, and I want to watch." He laughed at Elise's expression. "I can try to convince your aunt that you are telling the truth," he offered. "Unfortunately, not many big humans can see us clearly. I don't think your aunt would believe it even if she could see clearly."

They joined Neala in the cave and watched the passageway shimmer as she stepped through. Laisrén went next, and then Elise and Amos jumped through.

* * * * *

Whatever Elise expected to find as she came through the passageway, it was definitely not this. Neala was waving her sword at a very shocked Kevan Foley, who was sprawled on the ground next to the Faerie Ring. Laisrén was flitting around her and trying to explain who he was. Kevan was staring back and forth from the Gnome to the Fairy and kept swatting at Laisrén if he got too close.

"Everyone, stop it!" Elise shouted. "Neala, put your sword down. This is Kevan. He is the one we stole the stone—" she stopped mid-sentence and looked at Kevan guiltily.

"Aye," he agreed. "The one you stole the stone from. Lucky for you, I figured it out when your aunt called me this morning wondering if you'd been down to the store." He glared at Neala, who glared right back. Kevan grinned. "I'd been sitting there trying to figure out how the alarm had been turned off and a window unlocked from the inside when I saw the stone was gone. Nothing else was missing, and I was ready to call it the craziest robbery ever when your aunt called all worked up that you'd not been seen this morning, and your bag was gone and all. I remembered how you'd been in the back room yesterday and came up with the craziest idea about what you might be doing. I came here and found the stone but didn't dare move it in case you had actually gotten yourself stuck in the Faerie Realm. There were enough strange tracks around—and some blood, too— that I figured something unexpected had happened. If you hadn't come out soon, I was going to have to go in after you. And let me tell you," he added in a loud voice when Neala waved her sword, "that was something I had no keen desire to do, especially uninvited."

He looked at Laisrén, who had perched on his knee during this explanation. "You must be a Fairy then," he said, looking closely at him. "Never seen a male Fairy." He moved on to Neala. "You are no Elf," he said, considering. "You must be a Gnome. No Brownie would be waving a sword around at a human like that."

Neala lowered her sword. "If you know so much about us, why ever did you move the stone?" she demanded. "We were stuck here for weeks, and the Faerie Realm was nearly in shambles by the time we got back."

"I didn't know any Faerie were in this realm," he admitted. "I figured if any passageway really existed, it must have been broken ages ago when the stone was moved. I am sorry," he said sincerely.

Neala looked slightly mollified but then continued. "Well, since he's seen us, he may as well hear the rest. There are two Phookas loose here so be on the lookout for them. We will be back soon to take care of them." Amos barked and Neala actually smiled. "Yes. Unless Amos takes care of them first."

Kevan blinked. "You can understand him?" he asked hesitantly.

"Don't get her started," said Laisrén, rolling his eyes. "Next thing you know, she'll have a chat with all the plants just to show off."

Neala glared at him before turning her stern look on Kevan. "Don't move the stone," she commanded.

"Wouldn't dream of it," he said.

As Neala turned to go, another figure came out of the circle. It was Prince Rauri. He was closely followed by Tír.

"What is the problem?" Rauri asked. He looked at Kevan. "Is he causing trouble?"

Kevan blinked, staring at the new arrivals. "No trouble," Laisrén said. "He is the human we had to get our stone back from." He turned to Kevan with a smirk and announced in his grandest voice, "This is the Elf Prince Rauri and his servant, the Gruagacha magician, Tíreachán." He fluttered into the air and continued, "Elise can catch you up on everything else later. Let's get going. I want to see you try to explain everything to your aunt." He smirked at Elise and flitted back and forth in the direction of the house.

Neala bowed in Kevan's general direction, and he tried to bow back from his position on the ground. "See you later," she said to Elise as she jumped back into the circle and disappeared.

"Goodbye, Elise," Prince Rauri said, bowing to both her and Kevan. Tíreachán waved, and they both disappeared.

Kevan stared at Elise. "Elf prince? You're friends with an Elf prince?" he asked in awe. "And a magician?"

"And the princess. And I helped rescue the queen from an evil Gruagacha and traveled by rainbow." She smiled. "I've had a busy few days."

"It appears so," he agreed. "I can't wait to hear all about it."

"I promise I'll explain everything," Elise said. "But the biggest problem in this whole adventure is what to tell Aunt Mim. Is it really still the same day?" she asked in disbelief. "It's been days in the Faerie Realm."

Kevan nodded. "It's just after lunch, but your aunt has been all over town asking for you and has called me three times. Your uncle has been all through the woods, and everyone is really worried."

"What should I tell Aunt Mim?" Elise asked with a frown. "She will never believe that I was trapped in the Faerie Realm. She'll think I'm crazy."

"Aye," Kevan agreed. "Perhaps you could just say you were lost in the woods and not mention that the woods were in another realm. I'm not sure your aunt would believe you even if I swore you were serious." He stood up and brushed himself off. "I'm not sure I believe it, and I was knocked down by a two-foot Gnome with a sword." He shook his head again. "And she threatened to come back." He shuddered. "Amos will have to try to find those Phookas before that Gnome comes back."

Amos barked and started for the house. Elise picked up her bag and followed with Kevan, bracing herself for a long scolding. She sighed but then grinned as she saw a blue light fly past. At least Laisrén was going to enjoy this. She fingered the green stone in her pocket. If Aunt Mim got too worked up, she could always call for backup.

Appendix

Pronunciation:
The stress is always on the first syllable.

Rauri	Ro-ree
Turlach	Tur-la
Tíreachán	Teer-ach-awn
Meallán	Mel-awn
Laisrén	Las-rain
Líoch	Lee-ukh
Corc	Kur-uk
Murtagh	Mur-tah
Baoth	Bee
Fachtna	Facht-na

About the Author

Jess Jenkins was born and raised in northwest Pennsylvania. An English teacher by trade, she has lived in four different countries laboring (usually in vain) to convince students that grammar is exciting. On the weekend, she can usually be found in coffee shops or eating ice cream. *Elise and Amos and the Faerie Stone* is her first novel.

CPSIA information can be obtained
at www.ICGtesting.com
Printed in the USA
BVHW070047090320
574291BV00001B/6

9 781098 022136